## A Green Solution at Last?

If Stan heard me at all, he made no indication of it. He continued staring straight ahead, driving. Then, in one fluid move, he reached over, grabbed my phone—and hit the button to silence it.

My heart started beating faster in my chest. I leaned over, desperately pulling the handles on the door: locked. The other side was locked as well. I was trapped! Just then, Stan hit the gas, and the town car sped up.

He swerved right, and I realized that we were pulling onto a small industrial road. The road was deserted. The landscape was bleak and depressing, especially in the rain. But I knew there were at least a few companies still doing active business here.

Finally the car slowed, and we pulled up to an old brick building whose sign proclaimed that four businesses were located there. I scanned them and found what I was looking for right away: GREEN SOLUTIONS.

Not only was I interested in learning more about Green Solutions . . . they seemed to be pretty interested in learning more about *me*.

# NANCY DREW

**Available from Aladdin**

# CAROLYN KEENE

# NANCY DREW

GIRL DETECTIVE

## SEEING GREEN

**#41**

**Book Three in the
Eco Mystery Trilogy**

Aladdin

New York   London   Toronto   Sydney

❧ ALADDIN
An imprint of Simon & Schuster Children's Publishing Division
1230 Avenue of the Americas, New York, NY 10020
First Aladdin paperback edition April 2010
Copyright © 2010 by Simon & Schuster, Inc.
All rights reserved, including the right of reproduction in whole or
in part in any form.
ALADDIN is a trademark of Simon & Schuster, Inc., and related logo is
a registered trademark of Simon & Schuster, Inc.
NANCY DREW, NANCY DREW: GIRL DETECTIVE, and related logo are
registered trademarks of Simon & Schuster, Inc.
For information about special discounts for bulk purchases, please contact
Simon & Schuster Special Sales at 1-866-506-1949 or business@simonandschuster.com.
The Simon & Schuster Speakers Bureau can bring authors to your live event. For
more information or to book an event contact the Simon & Schuster Speakers Bureau
at 1-866-248-3049 or visit our website at www.simonspeakers.com.
Designed by Sammy Yuen Jr.
The text of this book was set in Bembo.
Manufactured in the United States of America
0210 OFF
10 9 8 7 6 5 4 3 2 1
Library of Congress Control Number 2009924061
ISBN 978-1-4169-7845-9
ISBN 978-1-4169-9910-2 (eBook)

# Contents

CAROLYN KEENE

# NANCY DREW

GIRL DETECTIVE®

## SEEING GREEN

**Book Three in the
Eco Mystery Trilogy**

# AIRPORT INSECURITY

If you had told me when my friends Bess Marvin, George Fayne, and I left for an all-expenses-paid vacation to Costa Rica that we wouldn't want to get on the plane to come back, I wouldn't have been surprised. But I wouldn't have been able to come *close* to imagining why!

"You feel guilty leaving, don't you?" Bess asked me as we tried to settle into our tiny airplane seats for the long flight back to Chicago. "After what happened to Sara . . ."

I sighed. "You know me, Bess," I said, reluctantly clicking my seat belt closed. "I hate to leave a mystery unsolved."

Maybe *unsolved* is the wrong word. *Partially solved* would be more accurate. See, when George won a vacation for two at the Casa Verde eco-resort in Costa Rica, she and Bess decided they couldn't leave me behind. So we split the cost of my plane ticket, and off we went—to the gorgeous, supposedly relaxing, supposedly "green" Casa Verde resort.

When we arrived, however, it became clear that we were about to get a little more than we bargained for. Almost as soon as we met our fellow vacationers, all journalists who were attending Casa Verde's press tour to celebrate its opening, things started to go wrong. At first, it was little things—stolen luggage, a dognapping. (The dog in question, Pretty Boy, was quickly recovered—and, in fact, was yapping away in first class with his owner as the three of us prepared for departure.)

But soon, it got more and more dangerous until people were narrowly avoiding getting hurt—yours truly included. After getting a little too up close and personal with an alligator, and finding out firsthand what happens when your zip line is cut (spoiler: you fall!), I was getting the feeling that someone at Casa Verde wanted us gone. And as it turned out, I was right. *Several* people at Casa Verde had things to hide: Among them, the fact that Casa Verde wasn't, well, quite so *verde* after all.

Casa Verde was billing itself as a state-of-the-art eco-resort, but in fact, all those fancy environmentally friendly fixtures and systems that were touted on their Web site were never actually installed. Instead, one of the brothers who owned the resort, Enrique Arrojo, had used substandard systems—and pocketed the money he saved. He claimed he was saving for his daughter Juliana's college education, but I was beginning to wonder if it was that simple.

One of his veterinary workers, Sara, had confessed to pulling the pranks that had made our stay so eventful—all to bring the journalists' attention to the ways Casa Verde was really hurting the environment it claimed to be protecting. She had claimed, though, that she *wasn't* behind the most dangerous stunts that had threatened me. And right before we left—right after confessing to Enrique and his brother Cristobal that she had sabotaged their press tour—she had been the victim of a poisonous ant attack!

I had so wanted to believe that Casa Verde's problems were over, but Sara's attack certainly made it look like *someone* is still holding a grudge.

"Look at it this way," George suggested, glancing up from her techie magazine. "At least when we get home, you can do some research on this Cassandra Samuels."

I nodded. Cassandra Samuels was the final ill-fitting piece of the puzzle. She worked for Green Solutions, the consulting firm that had supposedly advised Enrique and Cristobal on how to build an eco-friendly resort. And—more intriguingly—it seemed that she was Enrique's secret American girlfriend. Enrique's daughter Juliana had insisted to me that her father wasn't capable of all these scary attacks—that he *must* have had a co-conspirator, someone who had talked him into the scheme. At this point, if such a person existed, Cassandra Samuels seemed the most likely suspect.

"Oh . . . Em . . . Gee," a bubbly voice squealed in front of me, and then I heard a sharp *"Yip!"* and groaned. Bess, George, and I all turned to where Deirdre Shannon and her cousin, Kat, were coming down the aisle with Pretty Boy—Kat's precious, recently dognapped, extremely neurotic Chihuahua. Since Deirdre and Kat were traveling first class—Kat had paid to upgrade both their tickets—we hadn't been expecting to see them again until we landed. "Are you guys as happy to get on this plane as we are?"

Kat sighed, her platinum blond curls bobbing as she shook her head in exaggerated frustration. Kat lived in Los Angeles, and made her living working as an extra. She fancied herself an actress and, while nice enough, could be a bit overwhelming.

Bess smiled patiently. "We're glad to be getting home, for sure," she agreed. "Though we still have some unanswered questions."

"What do you mean?" asked Deirdre skeptically.

"Well," I said, "for instance, what happened to Sara?"

Kat shrugged. "You mean those ants?" she asked. "That stunk. But I guess those are the hazards you face working with animals. *Right, boobie-boo?*" She turned to Pretty Boy, cooing at a high pitch, and George gave me a desperate look, like *Make her stop!*

"Um," I said quickly. "Well, yeah . . . But it seemed like more than an accident to me, you know?"

Kat looked thoughtful. "You mean like when Pretty Boy was dognapped?"

"Yeah," George agreed, nodding. "Maybe someone was trying to send a message."

Kat stared off into space, seeming to think about this, but Deirdre didn't look convinced. "Either way," she snapped, "who cares? That was the worst vacation I ever took. Thank *goodness* we got it for free, otherwise I would be on the phone with my credit card right now, disputing the charges."

Kat glanced back at her cousin, then nodded. "Yeah," she agreed. "Whatever was really going on there, I'm just glad to be done with it."

Deirdre glanced at me. "Not *everyone* feels the need to snoop around in other people's business, Nancy. All I know is I'm going to kiss the ground when we get back to Chicago! I've had enough nature to last a lifetime."

George smirked. "Does that mean your environmental phase is over, Deirdre?" Before we'd left on our trip, Deirdre had claimed to "heart" the earth.

Now Deirdre sighed dramatically. "I suffered through a whole week with a low-flow showerhead," she complained, reaching up to grab a lank, dark lock of hair. "I think I'm all paid up on the environmental front for at least a year."

Just then, a flight attendant tried to make her way up the aisle, but paused behind Deirdre and Kat, who were blocking her. "Ladies," she said, "I'm afraid you'll need to take your seats. We're preparing for takeoff. And miss, your dog will have to return to its carrier and be placed under the seat."

"I know, I know." Kat rolled her eyes, hugging Pretty Boy close and glancing sideways at me. "I swear," she whispered after she and Deirdre had moved aside to let the stewardess through. "The way people treat Pretty Boy sometimes! It's like he's an *animal* or something. Well, ta!"

"Ta," echoed Bess, waving gamely. Then Kat and Deirdre disappeared behind the first-class curtain, and we settled in for our flight.

"Well," George said with a sigh, "I guess this is 'good-bye, Costa Rica.'"

I nodded, looking out the window at the gorgeous scenery with regret.

*Good-bye, Costa Rica,* I thought. *You'll be out of sight, but not out of mind.*

Back in Chicago a few hours later, Bess, George, and I stumbled out of the plane, cranky and sleepy-eyed. It was only mid-afternoon in Chicago, but after hours in the sky, it felt much later.

"Where do we go to get the bus to River Heights?" Bess asked, groggily searching the signs overhead. We'd all taken an express bus to the airport last week, and planned to return to River Heights, our hometown, the same way.

George playfully poked her arm. "We have to get our luggage first, ditz," she reminded her cousin. "Remember all your beloved clothes? Not to mention the bags and bags of souvenirs you brought home."

Bess shrugged. "I like to *remember* the experience, okay?"

I snorted. "Bess, I don't think you'll ever forget our week at Casa Verde."

We'd walked down the long terminal and now stepped onto the escalator that led down to baggage claim. We'd already said our good-byes to Kat, who was catching a connecting flight to L.A.; Deirdre had followed her to her new gate to see her off.

"Hey," George piped up, pointing lazily to the left as we stepped off the escalator. "Is that kinda weird?"

Bess rolled her eyes. "Is *what* kinda weird, George?" she asked, looking in the general direction George was pointing. "Cinnastix? Not really. They just use a lot of butter and—"

"*Not* Cinnastix," George insisted, grabbing her cousin's shoulder and spinning her to face what she was facing. "Those guys in the suits. Look at their signs."

I glanced at the men George was referring to. One was a pudgy Latino man in his forties or so; the other was tall, Caucasian, and bald, perhaps a little younger. Both were wearing dark suits and holding up signs, like dozens of car-service drivers who were waiting at baggage claim to pick up their charges. But George was right: There was something weird about these two.

Their signs read BESS MARVIN AND GEORGE FAYNE and NANCY DREW, respectively.

"Huh," I muttered, frowning at my friends. "You guys didn't arrange for car service, did you?"

Bess shook her head. "No way. To River Heights? That would have to cost hundreds of dollars."

George nodded in agreement. "Town-car service is too rich for my blood," she said. "I thought we were taking the *bus* home."

I nodded. "Me too."

"Well," said Bess, sighing as she shifted her purse to her other shoulder, "there's one way to get to the bottom of this." She began walking toward the suited men. "Excuse me? I'm Bess Marvin, and these are my friends George Fayne and Nancy Drew."

The two men nodded at Bess, and the one holding the sign with her and George's name smiled. "Pleased to meet you, Miss. We can just go help you retrieve your luggage and then be on our way."

Bess shook her head. "I'm sorry, I'm a little confused," she said. "We didn't arrange for any car service."

The taller man nodded. "Yes, but it's part of the prize package you won," he explained. "I believe it was an all-expenses-paid trip to Costa Rica?"

Bess turned to George and me, and we all exchanged skeptical looks.

"Um," I spoke up, "I don't think that was mentioned in any of the information we received. And we came *to* the airport by bus—if it were part of our prize, wouldn't it have applied both ways?"

The men looked confused, and the taller man reached into his inside jacket pocket. After a little digging, he fished out a folded computer printout. Unfolding it, he frowned and then nodded. "That's right. I'm sorry. This was arranged by a Mister Cristobal Arrojo, to make up for some difficulty you encountered during your stay."

*Hmm.* "Can I see that?" I asked, and the man politely handed it over. I looked down and read:

To: reservations@Apluscarservice.com
From: crarrojo@casaverde.com

Dear Sirs,
I would like to arrange a car service for three young ladies traveling from Chicago O'Hare to the town of River Heights. You will find their itineraries and addresses, as well as my credit card information, attached. They will not be expecting this service, so please seek them out. Please let them know that I have arranged for their comfortable journey home with deepest apologies for the difficulties of their stay. I am deeply grateful to all three girls for their assistance and their patience.
Sincerely,
Cristobal Arrojo

"Hmm," I murmured, looking over at my friends with a raised eyebrow.

"That definitely sounds like Cristobal," Bess said.

I nodded. "And this is his correct e-mail address," I added. "I remember from my . . . um . . ." *Snooping?* ". . . visits to his office." I looked down at the paper, then back up at my friends, whispering, "It's not an easy e-mail to guess . . . you know, since he has that extra *r* in there."

George nodded, seeming to accept this. "Well, that was nice of him."

"Definitely," agreed Bess. She turned back to the drivers. "Thanks so much—we just need to find our luggage now."

After a few minutes, we all figured out that our flight's luggage was being distributed at bay #4. Other passengers I recognized from the flight waited there, all looking as bored and ready to get home as we felt. After what seemed like forever, but was probably only a matter of minutes, Bess and George had both reclaimed their suitcases. Mine, however, was still missing—and the flow of new bags was slowing down. Most of our fellow passengers had already claimed their things and left.

"Uh-oh," I said with a sigh, after it had been a few minutes since the last bag had appeared. "Do you think they might have lost my bag, after everything else that went wrong on this trip?"

Bess sighed and shrugged. "Anything's possible, Nance," she said, looking sympathetic. "Here, we can come to the luggage office with you."

The shorter man cleared his throat uncomfortably. "Actually," he said, looking a little sheepish, "I have another pickup in ninety minutes. I don't want to rush you, but . . . if I could take Miss Marvin and Miss Fayne?"

Bess and George looked at each other, then to me, both wearing an expression of dismay.

"It's okay, guys," I assured them. "I'm sure this gentleman"—I pointed to the other, taller driver—"and I will be fine. If they lost my luggage, there's not much they can do right now, anyway. I'm sure they'll just send me home and send it out to me when it shows up."

Bess nodded, reaching in to give me a hug. "Get home safely, Nance," she said.

George leaned in to hug me too. "Thanks for coming," she added. "I know it wasn't quite the vacation we all had in mind."

I grinned. "Are you kidding? For Nancy Drew, no vacation is complete without a mystery to solve."

George laughed.

"I'm sure I'll be in touch soon," I promised. "You

know, with new thoughts on the case."

Bess nodded. "Sounds good, Nance. Talk to you then."

They disappeared out one of the doors leading to the parking lot, and I glanced up at my driver.

"Well, Miss," he said, looking around the baggage claim, "the baggage office for your airline seems to be over there. Shall we? My name is Stan, by the way."

I nodded and smiled. "Nice to meet you, Stan."

Together, we walked to the edge of the baggage claim area, where the small, glassed-in baggage office was positioned. Inside, we waited in line, then I gave the woman behind the counter all of my info—name, flight number, bag description, etc.

"If you'll have a seat," she said, gesturing to the plastic chairs that flanked the walls, "we'll be right with you."

I thanked her, and Stan and I took our seats. There was silence for a moment, and I felt awkward, so I blurted out, "Do you live in River Heights too, Stan?"

He glanced at me, looking surprised that I'd spoken to him. "No."

I nodded. "Do you, um . . . ," I began, searching for a good conversation starter. "Do you have any children?"

He frowned at me, still seeming a bit confused by

my attention, when his cell phone suddenly went off. He glanced down at the screen, then cupped it in his palm, hiding it from me. "Excuse me," he said. "I have to take this."

I nodded, and he stood up and walked out of the office and out of sight.

*Friendly guy,* I thought with a frown.

Just then, a woman in the bright-colored uniform of the airline we'd flown came over to me, dragging something behind her. "Miss Drew?" she asked.

"That's me," I confirmed, standing up.

She pushed the bag in front of her. I was happily surprised to see it was mine—blue with a red luggage tag. I smiled gratefully.

"I'm sorry, Miss Drew," she said, looking confused. "It seems that your bag has been here the whole time. Someone from the airline separated it from the other luggage and placed it here. I'm not sure why."

*Hmm.* "So it was never really lost?" I asked. That was unusual.

"It seems it never really was," she confirmed with a nod. Then she shot me a tired smile. "Anyway, I'm sure you must be relieved. You can head home now."

I nodded. "Thanks!"

I grabbed my suitcase and rolled it out of the office, wondering where Stan might have gone. There he was—several yards away, just out of sight of the baggage office, still on his phone. I caught his eye and smiled, gesturing to my suitcase, like *Yay!* If he was amused or relieved, though, he didn't show it. He continued speaking tensely into the cell phone, then abruptly shut it as I moved within earshot.

"It was here the whole time," I told him cheerfully. "Someone just grabbed it and put it in the baggage office. Weird, right?"

He nodded, but his expression didn't change at all. "Let's get going, Miss Drew," he said, taking the suitcase from me and briskly wheeling it down the corridor toward the exit.

I stood where I was for a moment, frowning. Stan seemed in an awful hurry to get going. Maybe he just had another pickup, like the other driver, but still . . . it was making the hairs on the back of my neck prickle. And that was always a telltale sign that something might be wrong.

"Hold on," I called, gesturing to the women's restroom to our left. "I'd just like to run in here first, please."

Stan turned around, not looking thrilled. He nodded impatiently. "Okay."

Leaving my suitcase with him, I darted into the bathroom and entered a stall, closing the door behind me. I fished my cell phone out of my pocket and sighed, then hurriedly dialed the number I'd memorized while in Costa Rica.

It rang three times. Then came the voice mail greeting. "Buenos dias, you have reached Cristobal Arrojo at Casa Verde. I'm unavailable right now. . . ."

I sighed. Okay, so I wasn't going to be able to get Cristobal to confirm this car-service plan. I left a quick message, and then locked my phone's keypad, suddenly aware of just how tired I was—not just from the flight, from the whole experience. For a week I'd been questioning everyone's motives, second-guessing every kindness, trying to get to the heart of what was going on in Casa Verde. Now I was home, and I was doing the same thing. Was I just being paranoid? Stan was probably just doing his job—it wasn't his job to be BFF with every passenger he ferried from place to place. It *was* his job to get them there in a timely manner, which probably explained his hurry.

Unlocking my phone again, I quickly texted Ned and my father:

GETTING INTO A CAR AT THE AIRPORT NOW, ON MY WAY HOME. MISS YOU!

Then I locked my phone once more, stood up, and walked out of the restroom.

"Okay," I said to Stan, when I found him standing against the wall outside, checking his watch. "I'm ready to go home now."

## TAKEN FOR A RIDE

It was raining outside, bathing the city in a gloomy wash of gray. Stan pulled a compact umbrella from his inside jacket pocket and expertly shielded me from the rain. I smiled at him gratefully. Once at the car—a sleek black town car with plush leather seats—he quickly threw my luggage in the trunk and settled into the driver's seat while I slid into the back.

"Have you lived in River Heights long?" he asked, once we were on the road. I answered, and slowly, we got into a normal conversation. He lived in Glenville, he explained, a small suburb of Chicago, with his wife and two kids. He usually loved driving, but days like today, with the rain and all, things got behind schedule and it all could be a little stressful.

I nodded understandingly. *So that's it,* I thought. *That's why he was a little tense at the airport. I really was being paranoid.*

We were traveling a familiar route home, and I relaxed a little, eager to see my dad and Hannah and Ned again. After a few minutes, my phone beeped and I glanced down to see a text from Ned:

CAN'T WAIT TO C U! MISSED U SO MUCH!

I smiled. Gosh, I had missed Ned, too. I wrote back:

IN THE CAR NOW ON THE HIGHWAY. SHOULD BE HOME IN ½ HOUR.

Stan turned on the radio, and I leaned back against the comfy seat, letting my mind wander as the rain-soaked landscape and the '60s tunes on the radio blended together. I closed my eyes for just an instant, and when I opened them again we were just an exit away from River Heights. I smiled. I was so close to home!

Stan picked up the transmitter to radio his dispatcher, but it didn't seem to be working. He kept pushing the button, calling out, "This is car forty-five, do you read me?" but no answer came. Finally, as we pulled off the highway and came to a stop at a stop sign with no one behind us, he put down the transmitter and turned around.

"This is awfully embarrassing," he said, "but my transmitter isn't working and I need to tell my dispatcher I'm about to drop you off. I switched off my cell when I got in the car—I don't like getting calls on the road—and it takes forever to turn on. Would you mind if I borrowed yours?"

I reached into my pocket to grab my phone, then paused. "Why isn't the transmitter working?" I asked. "Does that happen often?"

Stan sighed and nodded. "It's the rain," he said. "Yet another reason I hate rainy days. It screws up all our old equipment."

*Hmm.* I paused, my hand still on my cell phone. For just a second, that weird feeling I'd had in the airport returned—but then I thought it through. I'd *seen* the transmitter fail. And come to think of it, I had noticed him taking out his cell phone and shutting it off before we pulled out of the airport parking garage.

I pulled out my phone and handed it over. "Sure. Here you go."

Stan took the phone, smiled, and then pulled the car over to the side of the road. He clicked a button and a glass partition between the driver and the passenger seat slowly moved into place. I'd seen those before—they provide privacy to customers in limos or town cars. I was a little weirded out by his putting it up right then, but I figured he just wanted privacy.

Stan dialed, and after a moment, someone picked up and he started talking. I could only make out every few words through the glass. "Hi . . . wanted to . . . River Heights . . . dropping off Miss Drew . . ." Then he paused and laughed. ". . . Isn't working in the rain . . . five times." He laughed again. "Okay . . . off."

Clicking off the phone, Stan smiled and looked out through the windshield at the rain. I expected him to put down the partition and hand my phone back to me, but instead he placed the phone on the bench next to him and put the car in drive. Without a glance back at me, he pulled back up to the stop sign, then turned right, toward my house.

I shifted uncomfortably, but tried to stay calm. *You'll be home soon,* I told myself. *He probably just figures he'll give it back to you when he drops you off in five minutes.*

We kept driving, and at each intersection, Stan took the correct turn to get me home. I was beginning to relax again when suddenly I heard my phone ringing. I looked toward Stan, but he made no move to pick up my phone or give it back to me. He just kept driving. I pressed my face against the partition, struggling to look down and see whose number was flashing on the display screen.

*Cristobal's.* It was Cristobal calling me back!

"Hey!" I shouted, knocking on the partition. "Hey! I need my phone back, please! Someone's calling!"

But if Stan heard me at all, he made no indication of it. He continued staring straight ahead, driving. Then, in one fluid move, he reached over, grabbed my phone—and hit the button to silence it.

The tinny ring died all once.

And a horrible realization hit me:

*Why would eco-conscious Cristobal arrange for not one, but two gas-guzzling limos to take my friends and me home?*

I'd been duped!

My heart started beating faster in my chest. I leaned over, desperately pulling the handles on the door: locked. The other side was locked as well. I was trapped! Just then, Stan hit the gas, and the town car sped up. We were rocketing down a main street of River Heights, flanked by strip malls and shopping centers. He swerved to avoid a minivan, then bolted through a red light! He pulled into a grocery store parking lot, and a wave of relief washed over me—we were stopping! Maybe he was just getting directions! Maybe this would all be okay!

But then he swerved right, and I realized that we were pulling onto a small industrial road that ran behind the grocery store. He was still going fast, too fast for the small road, but we were the only ones on it as we sped away from the crowded shopping area, into River Heights' main industrial area, filled with crumbling old factories, active warehouses, and vacant lots.

We were still speeding, and the landscape changed quickly. The road was deserted now, no longer packed with minivans and SUVs. We were in a part of town few people ever found reason to visit. River Heights had once been a bustling manufacturing town, but much of this area had died off as more jobs were being sent overseas. The landscape was bleak and depressing, especially in the rain. But I knew there were at least a few companies still doing active business here.

Finally the car slowed, and we pulled up to an old brick building whose sign proclaimed that four businesses were located there. I scanned them and found what I was looking for right away: GREEN SOLUTIONS. It was the third from the top. I swallowed, trying to pull myself together.

Not only was I interested in learning more about Green Solutions . . . they seemed to be pretty interested in learning more about *me*.

And I had a feeling I was going to be meeting Cassandra Samuels a lot sooner than I thought.

## TRAPPED

**S**tan pulled the town car into the parking lot and came to a stop in one of the parking spaces that faced the low brick building.

I pounded on the glass partition, shouting, "Stan! STAN! I know you can hear me!" but he didn't respond.

After a few seconds, without even turning around to look at me, Stan opened the driver side door and climbed out. I watched as he walked from the car to the building, wordlessly opening and slipping inside a side door.

I was alone, in the car, in the rain.

And I was beginning to panic.

Just then, I was startled by a buzzing sound in the front seat. Leaning up to look through the glass partition, I realized it was my phone vibrating; Stan had left it on the front seat. Luckily, the display screen was facing up, so I could see BESS MARVIN flashing in the caller ID space. Bess was calling me! I moaned, pressing my nose against the glass, wishing I could get to my phone and tell Bess what was going on. Were she and George safe? Had their driver taken them to parts unknown too? Or was Green Solutions after only me?

I sighed as the buzzing sound died down, indicating Bess had given up. At least wherever she was, Bess still had her phone. That was a good sign.

I leaned over and tried the doors again: locked. Taking a deep breath, I pulled in my elbow and then rammed it, abruptly and with a lot of power, into one of the windows. *Ouch!* My elbow stung like crazy, but I hadn't even made a dent in the window. *Maybe they're made of unbreakable glass,* I realized. If this car was often used for transporting people against their will, that would make sense.

I sat for a moment, trying to collect my thoughts. *Cassandra Samuels.* If that was really who was waiting for me inside, then I was in real trouble. At Casa Verde, *someone* had tried to kill me more than once— by cutting my zip line, and by trying to push me overboard into a river full of alligators, among other ways. If Cassandra was really behind that—if, in fact, Green Solutions had *anything* to do with that—that meant they were willing to kill me. If that was the case, who knew what awaited me inside that brick building?

My heart pounded in my chest, echoing in my ears. I *had* to get out of this car. It was my only hope of getting out of this in one piece!

But *how*?

My pulse still racing, I tried to think. I was in an Abrahams town car; I'd noticed the make before climbing in. I tried to channel Bess, summoning every random piece of gearhead trivia she'd ever told me. (Bess was a gearhead of the highest order.) How could I get out of a Abrahams town car when I'd been locked inside? Was there a way to jimmy the lock from within? Any kind of secret release button that would free me?

I couldn't think of anything. The car seemed pretty solid: the sort of car people invested in and kept for a long time. Not the sort of car you could pry open with a nail file, or anything else I might have at my disposal.

I sighed, looking down at my purse. It contained barely anything that might help me. Not for the first time, I cursed myself for not being the type to travel with pliers, a hammer, or some sort of skeleton key. All I had was my worn wallet, some tissues and a lip gloss Bess had insisted on my buying and carrying around—she said it "lit up my face."

If only it would launch me out of this car!

Then, suddenly, I looked down at the bench my purse was sitting on; it was leaning against the armrest that divided the back seat to accommodate two passengers. That's when I remembered something Bess had told me. Leaning closer, I ran my hand over the smooth leather of the armrest and back toward the padded bench—into the small, rectangular compartment the armrest folded into to make room for a third passenger.

The compartment was small, bordered on three sides by the leather back cushion of the bench.

The far wall of the compartment, though, was just made of felt.

I remembered something Bess had explained to me once: this little compartment, basically just a hole in the passenger seat, led straight back into the trunk.

And in most modern cars, there would be a release lever in the trunk to avoid anyone getting stuck in there.

I felt my heart speeding up. *This could be it!* If I could somehow squeeze myself through that space and get into the trunk . . .

I started digging in my purse. Tissues, nail file, keys—*bingo!* My house key had a sharp, jagged edge that, when applied with enough force, would easily cut through felt.

Wrapping the key in my right hand, I jabbed at the felt behind the armrest.

It took some serious pushing, but eventually the key broke through to the other side.

I glanced up at the building. Was Stan coming back? He had to be, eventually. I assumed he was in the warehouse letting Cassandra Samuels know I was out there; sooner or later, I would be retrieved from the car and taken inside. Or worse—a chill ran down my spine at the thought—Stan would come back and transport me somewhere else where I'd be "dealt with."

I couldn't let that happen! With renewed vigor, I kept pounding the key into the felt—finally tearing off a flap just big enough for me to grab in my fist and pull back into the car. Yanking as hard as I could, I tore away the remaining felt and pulled it out, dropping it onto the car floor and peering into the dark hole I'd opened up.

The hole was tiny, but there was no denying it: It definitely led into the car's trunk. In the gray mid-afternoon light that filtered in from the backseat, I could just barely make out the edges of my suitcase inside.

I took a deep breath. Would I be able to squeeze myself through?

Climbing onto all fours on the bench, I leaned my head closer to the opening, finally pushing it inside and into the trunk. It was pitch black in there, especially with my body blocking the afternoon light. But I had just about enough space to squeeze my shoulders through—if I shifted my body so they were coming through vertically.

No longer able to see anything, I paused, waiting to see if I heard a door opening or any evidence of Stan coming back. I didn't. As hard and fast I could, I pushed the rest of my body through the hole I'd created. It wasn't easy—I had to suck in worse than I'd ever had to to fit into a pair of jeans—but I made it.

A few seconds later, I was crouched inside the dark, tiny space of the trunk.

Reaching out my hand, I began feeling along the metal walls for the trunk release. I struggled to maneuver around my suitcase in the small space, taking deep breaths to try to slow my pounding heart. *Don't panic!* I told myself as the first pass over the perimeter didn't reveal the trunk release. *Just keep going . . .*

Finally, I felt it. It was on my left, over where I imagined the bumper of the car being. A small, plastic handle. I grabbed it and pulled with all my might, and immediately, the trunk *click*ed and floated open.

I blinked, blinded by what suddenly seemed like super bright light . . . and then wiped furiously at my eyes as rain dropped into them. Pushing the trunk completely open, I pushed myself up to my knees and looked around. The parking lot was still silent. I had a chance! Gasping for air, I scrambled out of the trunk, forcing my legs down onto the pavement. Once upright again, I started running—faster and less gracefully than I ever had before.

At the edge of the parking lot, the door to the building opened, and then I heard the gasp: "You! Where are you going?"

But by then I had a head start. My legs churning like pistons, I ran out of the parking lot and down the street, praying that something—anything—would be open.

There wasn't much on the industrial road that I could use, and soon I heard the town car's engine starting up—Stan was going to chase me in the car. I darted behind a building, running into an overgrown field and across it, zigzagging into the parking lot of the building on the block behind. I was still in a depressed industrial area, and everything seemed to be closed. I ran behind another warehouse, onto some abandoned railroad tracks, then along them.

Squinting in the rain, I saw it: a tiny corner deli situated in a run-down corner shop connected to a catalog shipping center. The old-fashioned 7 Up ad on its sign caught my eye.

It was lit up.

The place might be open!

Gasping for breath, panting from exhaustion, I ran over to the deli and climbed the two worn steps to the front door. I pulled the door open, a sad jingling alerting the workers that I was there.

Two dark-haired Latino men sat behind a counter, watching a soccer game on a tiny black-and-white television.

"I need to use your telephone," I said, wheezing for air. "It's an emergency!"

A few seconds later, I was tapping my foot impatiently, feeling my heart pound faster with each ring.

Finally Ned's voice answered, so warm and familiar I might have cried. "Hello? Who is this?"

"It's me, Ned," I said, relief flooding every cell in my body. "And I'm in trouble. I need you to come pick me up ASAP."

# A DANGEROUS PROMISE

"This is really scary, Nance," Bess told me with wide eyes as we sat piled with Ned and George on my living room couch. In the kitchen, my father was on the phone with the River Heights Police Department. He was seriously, seriously freaked out about this abduction attempt, if that's what it was, and he was trying to convince the police that they needed to give me protection. From the sound of it, they were being typically reluctant. I've dealt with the River Heights police a lot—they're not bad guys, but sometimes they're a little slow to pick up on a serious threat.

"*Very* scary," agreed Ned, taking my hand for

the third time and squeezing it. "You looked really frightened when I picked you up at that deli, Nance. And you don't get frightened that easily."

I swallowed. Ned was right—the whole incident in the town car had really shaken me. I think, with all the experience I've had sleuthing and getting myself in trouble, I've learned to tell a fake threat from a real one. And that car ride was really, really dangerous. If I hadn't been able to break out of the car . . .

Well.

I wouldn't be sitting *here,* that's for sure.

A few minutes ago, my friends and I had gone into my dad's office to look up A Plus Car Service on the Internet. Not surprisingly, it appeared that no such service existed. We'd agreed that most likely, Green Solutions had hired the drivers to get me alone—and delivered to their warehouse.

*Shudder.*

We'd also tried calling Cristobal again, on Bess's cell. No answer. We'd left her number and a quick message, imploring him to call us back ASAP.

Now I cleared my throat. "I know," I said, "and honestly, yeah, I was pretty frightened. But the important thing is that I got away, and now I'm safe at home. If my dad succeeds, soon we'll have a police car sitting outside, guarding the house. And once we get to the bottom of this, I'll be out of danger."

George glanced toward the kitchen, where my father's voice was booming: "... *attempted kidnapping, Hank!* You can't tell me the RHPD doesn't take that seriously...."

"You really think he'll convince him?" she asked, turning to me with a cocked head.

I smiled. "George, sometimes it's handy to have the number one lawyer in the state as your father."

Bess chuckled. Just then, we all jumped as a top 40 dance tune came blaring from the couch cushions. Bess reached for the source—her phone—and glanced at the display screen. Then she quickly held it to her ear, giving us all a meaningful look. "Oh, hello, *Cristobal*. Thank you so much for calling us back! I think Nancy wants to talk to you...."

She shoved the phone at me, and I held it to my ear, feeling caught off guard. "Hello?"

"Nancy?" Cristobal's warm, accented voice came through the line. "I got both of your messages. Are you okay? I was worried that something happened."

"Oh, I'm okay . . . now," I added awkwardly. "Cristobal, I need to ask you something. Did you arrange for car service for the three of us from the airport?"

There was a pause, as I assumed Cristobal was thinking it over. "Car service?" he said finally. "No. Nancy, you know public transportation is better for the environment! That's why Casa Verde—"

I didn't want to be rude, but I interrupted to keep him from going off on this tangent. "I know, Cristobal. I know. I just . . . wanted to check."

Cristobal seemed to accept this. "*Sí*. Well, to be honest, Nancy, I wouldn't have been able to arrange a car service for you even if I'd wanted to. Things have been a little *loco* since you left."

"They have?" I asked, glancing at my friends with a frown. "Crazy how?"

He sighed. "You remember what happened to Sara before you left. . . . She put on the hat that had been filled with biting ants."

"Yes," I agreed. The memory of Sara in pain, jumping into the pool to dissuade the biting bugs, definitely stuck with me. "Is she okay?"

"No," replied Cristobal, shortly. "A few hours after you left, Sara began to feel sick, with a high fever. It turned out one of the bites had become infected. We took her to the hospital, where she is on antibiotics and doing better. But when I went to tell Enrique . . ."

Cristobal trailed off, as though the memory pained him.

"What happened?" I prompted, gripping the phone in my hand as my friends gave me curious looks. "What happened to your brother when you told him Sara was sick?"

"I . . . don't know," Cristobal admitted, sounding exhausted and sad. "The doctors at the hospital . . . they say it is a nervous breakdown."

I felt my heart quicken. *What?* "What do you mean, Cristobal? What happened?"

"He became very upset, heart pounding, hyperventilating. My wife, she says—she thought it was a panic attack. But we try to calm him down, and we cannot. He's still hyperventilating. He started to cry," Cristobal went on. "In the end, we took him to the hospital. They gave him medicine, and he calmed down."

That was a relief. "So he's better now?" I asked.

Cristobal laughed—a sad laugh. "That depends who you ask," he said. "He feels better, and is not panicking, yes. But now . . . he refuses to speak. Not to me, not to my wife, not to Juliana, his own daughter. Not to anyone."

I tried to absorb that. Enrique was that upset by Sara's illness?

There was only one emotion strong enough to produce a response like that, I figured.

Guilt!

"Oh," Cristobal said suddenly, "hold on. Juliana is here. We just came home to get some dinner before we go back to the hospital. But she wants to talk to you. Here . . ."

"Wait!" I called. I hadn't had a chance to tell Cristobal what happened with the car service, or to make sure, once and for all, that he knew nothing about it. But before I could get his attention, Juliana's voice filled the line.

"Nancy?" she said. "Is it really you?"

"It's really me," I affirmed. "Juliana, are you okay? This must have been a really tough afternoon."

Juliana was quiet for a minute, but then she spoke. "You see now, don't you, Nancy?" she asked finally. "My father couldn't have done this. He's not the type of person who would ever hurt anybody. He had to be set up by someone else . . . and now the guilt is destroying his health."

I bit my lip. I had to admit . . . my gut said that Juliana was right.

"You agree, don't you?" Juliana prodded, after a few seconds went by without my responding. "You know my father, Nancy. You know I'm telling the truth."

I sighed. "Juliana . . . what you're saying makes sense."

I could hear the satisfaction in her voice as Juliana went on, "*Bueno.* Then you'll agree, Nancy: You have to find Cassandra Samuels. You have to make her tell you the truth."

I gulped again. I believed Juliana, Cassandra was

the axis of the whole plot . . . but she'd also tried to kidnap me! Really, she might have been trying to kill me. My father was on the phone right now, trying to get police to guard our house to keep this woman away from me. How could I go after her now?

"Juliana," I said, "it's not that simple. It's become much more dangerous here. I believe Cassandra tried to kidnap me today—"

"So you see yourself!" Juliana cried, cutting me off. "Nancy, she's a criminal. Who knows what she'll do to my father if he tells the truth? And if he doesn't tell the truth about what Cassandra made him do, then he'll take all the blame. Nancy, *please.* I know you have a heart. I know you care about my family."

I was quiet, taking a deep breath. Of course Juliana was right. Of course I'd come to care about all of the Casa Verde owners and employees while we'd been there . . . but especially Cristobal, Enrique, and Juliana.

"*Please,* Nancy," Juliana went on, dropping her voice to barely above a whisper. "My family's future depends on it. Tell me you'll find Cassandra Samuels, and make her pay."

I closed my eyes. But no matter what I told myself, I couldn't keep the words from coming out: "I promise," I whispered.

"*Thank you,*" Juliana said, her voice infused with

warmth again. "Nancy, I have to go. Cristobal and I have finished eating. We need to get back to the hospital. My father is refusing meals, and we need to convince him to eat."

I sighed. It was unbelievable what poor Juliana's family was going through. "Okay."

"We'll talk soon, yes?" Juliana asked. "Good-bye, Nancy. I feel better knowing you are on the case."

"Good-bye."

I heard the phone click, then took Bess's phone away from my ear and pressed the End button.

Six anxious eyes fixed on me, demanding that I tell them what had happened.

I leaned in close. "Guys, we have to get away from my father," I whispered, glancing toward the kitchen, "because I'm about to hatch a plan he would never approve of in a million years."

# SECRET PLANS

A half hour later, the four of us were sitting around the computer in my bedroom. "Okay," said George, picking up the notes she'd been taking and turning from the computer screen. "So far we've found out that Green Solutions is a top-rated company, responsible for building eco-friendly resorts and buildings all over the world. They're responsible for Casa Verde, of course, but also for resorts in Hawaii and Malibu, a new baseball stadium in Florida, the New York headquarters of a huge publishing company, even several celebrities' mansions. And yes, they are headquartered right in downtown Chicago."

I nodded. "Which is *not* far from us at all," I added. That was important to my plan.

George went on, "Plus—they do have a small warehouse space in River Heights, Nance, which is on Burrell Drive, in the industrial area behind the mini-malls where you were taken." She paused, looked up at me, and swallowed hard. "Which makes it seem ever more likely that Green Solutions was behind that car ride. They wanted to get you to that showroom, and . . ." She sighed and trailed off.

Ned and Bess exchanged pained looks.

"It's okay," I insisted. "I'm okay now. Whatever they planned, they didn't succeed."

George nodded a little too hard, like she was trying to convince herself, and continued, "On their Web site, that warehouse is described as a 'showroom for some of our green fixtures and building materials.' And according to the same site, it seems they have relatively few employees. The only employees listed are Cassandra Samuels, CEO, a financial officer, and two assistants."

"Great," I said, leaning in and looking around at all my friends. "The fewer employees they have, the easier it will be to pull this off."

Bess frowned. "Pull *what* off?" she asked, looking back at the site on my monitor with fresh concern. "Nance, you keep hinting like you want to go after

Cassandra yourself. But she might have tried to *kill* you—she might even be behind some of what happened in Costa Rica! You don't seriously think you should confront her?"

I bit my lip. Bess seemed to read my hesitation, and began, *"Nance—"*

"*I* don't want to confront her," I interrupted, rushing out the words, "but we need to get into that headquarters, guys! We need to hunt for evidence. I really feel like Green Solutions could be behind everything—the cover-up at Casa Verde, all the scary events there, *everything*! But right now, I can't even come close to proving that. And the one person who could tell us the truth about Green Solutions— Enrique—isn't talking."

There was silence for a moment as my friends took that in. I'd filled them in on my phone call with Cristobal and Juliana as soon as we'd gotten to my room.

Finally Ned spoke. He looked directly at me as he said gently, "Nance, don't you think that's meaningful? If they have Enrique in such a state—if he's *that* scared—don't you think that tells us something about how dangerous this company is?"

I sighed, shifting my weight. "Of course, you're right," I said, shrugging. "But we don't have a choice, Ned. If we want to solve this case—and stop people from being hurt—we have to get our information straight from the source."

There was silence for a moment. Ned sighed again and crossed his arms in front of his chest. I was familiar with this stance—it was his *I don't know, Nancy* look. As unconvinced as he seemed, I knew this was a good sign—it meant he was thinking over the idea, and soon he would see it my way.

"So how do we do it?" Bess asked, looking thoughtful. "Obviously, Green Solutions knows what you look like—and they probably know what George and I look like too, from the drivers they sent. So *we* couldn't go to their offices."

"Exactly," I replied, looking over at Ned. "*We* couldn't go. . . ."

Ned, who had uncrossed his arms and seemed to be moving into his *well, maybe . . .* stance, suddenly backtracked. "Oh, no," he said, frowning as he met my gaze. "No, no, no, no . . ."

"*Ned,*" I coaxed. "Come on. You see how important this is. *I* almost got hurt, but Enrique, Juliana, Cristobal, and Sara—they're suffering right now! And I think that may be all because of Green Solutions."

Ned sighed. "I get that, Nance," he said, "but listen— I'm not you. I'm no kind of sleuth. I don't know how to take *fingerprints* or question *perks* or whatever."

I tried to stifle my smile. "I think you mean *perps*," I said, "but that's really more the police department's thing. We would just need you to go in undercover— as a prospective client."

Ned's eyes widened. "A prospective *client*?" he asked. "But I'm just a student! I don't even know where my suit is."

I shook my head. "That's okay, Ned. Look, you're the only one of the four of us that looks anywhere *close* to old enough to pass as a client. And if we clean you up, and slick back your hair, and you wear a nice dress shirt and pants . . ." I smiled. "Presto! Businessman. I thought we could say you were a bigwig from the university, looking for someone to help them build an eco-friendly dorm."

Ned leaned back in his chair, still looking unconvinced. "That's great," he said, "until I open my mouth. I'm a *terrible* actor. I won't know what to say to pull this off."

George leaned in, shrugging her shoulders. "You don't have to be fantastic," she pointed out. "You would just need to fool them long enough for us to sneak in and start searching their offices."

Ned looked thoughtful. I glanced over at George and gave her a quick thumbs-up, glad she liked my plan.

"Okay," Ned said finally. But he didn't look happy

about it. He was staring at a spot on my rug, his expression faraway.

"Oh, *thank you!*" I squealed, jumping up to give him a hug. "You'll see, Ned. It will all work out. We'll prep you really well. I'm sure George can help us mock up some documents and fake facts and figures to take with you."

George nodded. "Sure thing. In fact, I can start right now."

We spent the next couple of hours refining our plan. George created an impressive array of documents that we placed in an old leather binder of Dad's. We came up with a fake name for Ned— Carson Marvin—that would be easy for him to remember. And we planned for Ned to call Green Solutions the next morning from his work-study job (all the University phone numbers had the same exchange). He would set up an appointment after normal business hours, since Green Solutions' Web site emphasized that they "catered to the busy businessman," and we figured we'd have an easier time sneaking into the office if most employees had gone home.

When I finally looked at my watch, it was past ten o'clock. "Wow," I breathed. "It's getting late!"

Bess looked at her watch and frowned. "Oh, man. I'd better get going."

George glanced at the computer and saved the sheet she was working on. "Me too," she added.

"Me three," said Ned.

I walked my friends downstairs, excited and a little nervous about the next day. Ned promised to call us all as soon as he had the appointment set up. And they all agreed to come back to the house at four to prep for our meeting.

Bess and George said their quick good-byes and headed out to Bess's car, while Ned lingered on my doorstep.

"Thank you," I told him seriously. "I know this makes you uncomfortable. But you'll be great."

Ned nodded, then suddenly looked behind me and widened his eyes.

"Be great at what?" my father asked, walking up behind us with a big smile.

"Oh, ah . . . just something at school." Ned shrugged. He really was a terrible liar.

I turned to my dad with a smile. Normally I hate lying to him, but in this case I knew I had no choice. "Ned has a big history test tomorrow," I explained. "He's a little nervous."

My father faked shock. "Nervous about a test?" he asked, playfully tapping Ned on the shoulder. "I thought my daughter was dating a genius! A star student!"

Ned smiled warily. "Well, I try. Good night, Nancy. Good night, Mr. Drew."

My father nodded at Ned, and he walked down the path toward his car, which he'd parked on the street.

"See that?" whispered my father. I was so absorbed in watching Ned leave, at first I thought he was talking about Ned, but then I turned and followed his pointed finger to a River Heights PD patrol car sitting across the street.

"Dad!" I cried with a smile. "You convinced them!"

My father chuckled. "Well, partly. They still think the incident with the car was a misunderstanding and they're not planning to investigate further. But I worked the old Carson Drew magic on them, and they agreed to keep an eye on you for twenty-four hours."

With a relieved sigh, I grabbed my father's hand and gave it a squeeze. "*Thank* you," I said. "Really. Dad, you're amazing."

He nodded, his eyes turning serious. "Nance, you know I would do anything to keep you safe."

A few seconds later he walked back into the house, saying he had some paperwork to catch up on, but I lingered on the front stoop for a while, watching the officers watch me from the car across the street. After a moment, I gave a hesitant, friendly wave, and both officers waved back.

My throat caught and I walked back inside.

What kind of daughter was I? My father was doing everything he could to keep me safe ... and the next day, I was planning to walk right into the office of the woman I believed was trying to hurt me.

# 6

# OPERATION DISTRACTION

*Rrrring! Rrring!* I was woken up the next morning by the phone by my bed, its old-fashioned ring burrowing into my dreams. After a few moments of confusion, I jumped up in bed and grabbed the receiver, glancing quickly at the caller ID screen.

NANCY DREW.

Wait . . . *I* was calling me?

"Hello?" I answered, realizing all at once that this had to be a call from my cell phone—that Stan, or whoever had ended up with it, was on the other end of the line. "Hello?" I asked again, after a few seconds. "Who is this?"

The voice that finally came over the line sent a chill up my spine. It was deep and robotic—clearly disguised. No real human being sounded this creepy.

"Good morning, Nancy."

I felt my heart speeding up. "Who is this?" I demanded again.

The voice went on, as though the person hadn't even heard me: "You got away from us this time, Nancy Drew—but you can't keep running forever."

*Click.* The other person hung up, and I soon heard the dial tone ringing in my ear.

I shuddered, placing the phone back and swinging my feet over the side of my bed. *Don't think I'll get back to sleep after that.*

A four o'clock, I said good-bye to my dad and sauntered outside to the patrol car parked in front of our house. The car had changed over a couple times—the officers inside weren't familiar—but I still smiled warmly as I approached the driver's side window.

"Hi," I said to the officers inside. "I'm heading over to my boyfriend's dorm at the university to hang out for a little bit. Is that okay?"

The officer in the driver's seat—Officer Yang, his badge told me—shrugged and smiled. "It's fine with us. You're in charge, Miss. But you still have six hours of protection to go. Shall we follow you in your car?"

I nodded, relieved. "Great. It's the Prius right over there. I'll just be a minute."

Walking to my car, I felt butterflies in my stomach. My being under police protection sure put a wrinkle in our plans to drive to Chicago and sneak into Green Solutions, which I was pretty sure was illegal, strictly speaking. Ned had called earlier today to confirm that he'd called Green Solutions and spoken to Cassandra herself. When he'd laid out some of the information George had made up for him, Cassandra had told him she was *very* interested in meeting with him, and offered to make time tonight at 7 p.m.

"What did she *sound* like?" I'd whispered to Ned, standing in the corner of our kitchen as my dad ate his breakfast a few yards away.

"I'm not sure," Ned had admitted, sounding thrown by the question. "She sounded . . . normal. Friendly. Businesslike. Not at all like an environment-destroyer, killer, or kidnapper."

I frowned. I wasn't sure what I'd wanted Ned to say—I knew from my own experience that crooks often looked like perfectly normal, upstanding members of society. Still, I wasn't sure what to make of this woman who'd almost (I was pretty sure) kidnapped me. It was strange to think of her just going about her business, making deals with hapless university bigwigs.

"Well, anyway," I'd gone on, "we're on for tonight at seven, right?"

"Right," agreed Ned. "So I'll see you here for Operation Distraction at four thirty."

Now I pulled cautiously out of my driveway and started the twenty-minute drive to Ned's dorm at the university. If we wanted to make it to Chicago tonight, I had to lose the River Heights PD. I felt a little bad plotting to evade them when my dad had gone to such great lengths to secure their protection, but I felt it was the only way. Once we'd searched the Green Solutions offices and found some evidence, I kept telling myself, we could get to the bottom of this and let the authorities take care of them then.

Once at the university, I parked in the visitor's lot and walked over to the patrol car again. Officer Yang rolled down the window.

"I'll be in that dorm, right there," I said, gesturing to Seaver Hall.

Officer Yang nodded, taking the keys out of the ignition and nodding to his partner. "We'll come with you," he said. "If you're going to be surrounded by people, we should really be there to keep an eye out. You know, it's one thing to leave you in your house with your dad, but a different story with a whole bunch of strangers."

I swallowed hard and nodded. This wasn't exactly a surprise. I knew the RHPD weren't wild about the idea of protecting me, but they were professionals. They would try to do their best.

Together, Officer Yang, his partner, Officer Heller, and I walked into Seaver Hall. I checked in at the front desk, and soon Ned came out to greet me, smiling broadly. "Hey, Nance," he said happily, before taking note of the officers behind me. "Oh," he said. "You brought company."

Officer Yang grinned. "Don't worry," he promised, "we'll give you some privacy. But I'm sure Ms. Drew told you we're protecting her until this evening."

Ned nodded. "Sure," he agreed. "And that's a good thing."

Ned led us up to his room, pointing out the common lounge area that sat at the end of the hallway, a couch facing the corridor of dorm rooms. "Maybe you guys could hang here?" he asked with a hopeful smile, glancing at the police. "I don't honestly know if the four of us would fit in my room. . . ."

Officer Heller smiled. "This will be fine," he

confirmed, settling on the couch and grabbing the remote. "Just keep the door open."

Ned nodded. "Sure. Of course."

I followed him down the corridor to his room, the third door on the left. Once inside, he nodded at me, I nodded back, and he picked up his phone and dialed.

"Sunil," he whispered into the phone, "popcorn! Now!" There was a pause, and Ned looked at me, a little confused. "I don't know. Maybe ten minutes?"

I nodded.

"Ten minutes," Ned confirmed. Then he put down the phone, and we sat down, him on his bed, me on his desk chair.

"Now," I said, looking out into the hallway with an impatient sigh, "we wait."

So we did. It was only a couple minutes before we heard the familiar *bang bang bang!* of popcorn popping in the microwave in the common room. Then a cell phone rang, and someone answered it, walking out of the common room as he talked. Little by little, the *bang* sounds slowed down as the popcorn finished popping. But the microwave kept going. After a few minutes I heard Officer Yang ask, "Do you smell that?"

*I* could smell it. The bag of popcorn Sunil had

placed in the microwave was burning, just as Ned had arranged before I'd gotten there. And just as we'd hoped, someone was walking across the common room now, and soon they opened the microwave door—freeing a whole bunch of trapped smoke, and setting off the dorm smoke detectors.

*BEEP! BEEP! BEEP! BEEP! BEEP!*

Ned looked at me with a triumphant grin, and I smiled back. *Success!*

Already, chaos was spreading through the dorm, as students threw open their doors and ran into the hall.

"What the *heck*?"

"Omigod, not popcorn again!"

"Who did it? Oh, man, was it those *cops*?"

"Oh no! What are cops doing here, anyway? Is someone in trouble?"

After a moment, Ned poked out his head, then turned and nodded to me. On light feet, we snuck out the door, and I threw a quick glance down the hall to the common room. At least twenty or thirty students were blocking the officers' view—and Sunil, who'd strolled back in with his cell phone in hand, was shouting indignantly, *"What happened to my popcorn? That was my dinner, guys!"*

Ned grabbed my hand, and I followed him down the hall to the back staircase. We ran down to the main floor, then down one more flight, to a fire exit that let you out on a path that led to a dining hall. The door had an alarm, but since the fire alarm was going off anyway, nobody would notice. We ran down the path to the dining hall—and then around the side of the building, to a small, little-known parking lot where Ned had left his car.

"All right," he announced, settling into the driver's seat as I scrambled in next to him. "Operation Distraction was a success. Chicago, here we come!"

We picked up Bess and George along the way, and about an hour later, we pulled up in front of Green Solutions' main offices.

"Wow," George muttered, staring out the window. "This is totally not what I pictured."

"Me neither," I admitted.

In my mind, Green Solutions was always housed in a sparkly new building, maybe glass, and totally state-of-the art and eco-friendly. In real life, though, they were located in a quaint older neighborhood, surrounded by other prewar buildings. The building where Green Solutions was located on the eighth floor looked to be from the early twentieth century, and was boxy, dirty red brick. Gargoyles scowled at us from the top eaves of the building. I sighed.

"It's not very big," I observed, "which means it

won't be all that easy to sneak in four people at seven o'clock at night."

Bess frowned, taking in the building. "There's gotta be a way," she insisted. "Anyway, that's why we came early, right? To come up with a plan."

"Right," I agreed. "All right, let's check it out."

In the end, what saved us was the dermatologist's office on the fourth floor. When you entered the building, a tired-looking receptionist greeted you and asked you to sign in and write down the office you were going to. Then she would call the office and make sure you were really headed up there. What the four of us learned from secretly observing a few visitors, however—of course out of sight of the receptionist's wary eyes—was that the dermatologist's office never answered their phone. Each time, the receptionist would sigh, roll her eyes, and finally say to whoever was waiting, "Go ahead up." She never called back or seemed to check whether the patient had made it up there.

*Perfect.*

"We're here for Dr. Visnaya," Bess announced about half an hour after we'd arrived in Chicago.

"Both of you?" asked the receptionist warily, glancing from Bess to George, who stood beside her.

"This is my cousin," Bess replied, looking a little

insulted by the receptionist's question. "She's here for *moral support!* My acne medication hasn't been working."

The receptionist just stared at Bess, who happens to have perfect skin. "All right. Sign in," she instructed, then picked up the phone. As expected, a few minutes later she just sighed and passed them up.

About forty minutes later—so we wouldn't make the receptionist suspicious when lumped in with the dermatologist's *real* patients—I walked up. "I'm here to see Dr. Visnaya, please."

The receptionist nodded. "Sign in please. Your name?"

"Um, Nancy Drew."

I realized the moment the name left my lips that I'd messed up—I hadn't meant to give my real name! I just hoped it wouldn't work against me somehow.

The receptionist was already on the phone. She waited, her eyes bored, and then suddenly perked up. "Oh, *hello!*" she said, sitting up in her chair and flashing me a smile. "Fancy talking to you today. Listen, this is Maria downstairs and I have a patient for you—a *Nancy Drew?* Can I send her up?"

I felt my pulse quickening. This was the first time the dermatologist's office had answered their phone all day! Why, *why* did it have to be when I was trying to sneak in?

The receptionist was already scowling. I clutched my purse, wondering if I'd have to run out of there. And if I did, how would I get back in? The receptionist would be looking out for me now. I'd have to break in somehow—hope someone had left a window open, or that Bess and George could open a fire exit for me.

"No," the receptionist said now, "*Nancy Drew,* not Miranda Donald. *Nancy Drew.*" Finally she sighed, said, "Whatever" into the receiver, and hung up, giving me a disgusted look.

"I swear," she said to me, "they don't know *what's* going on up there. You go on ahead."

I smiled, passing by her and into a waiting elevator. *I'd done it!* Sometimes it paid to be young and innocent-looking. And to have the occasional pimple, I guessed.

I met Bess and George on the eighth floor, where, after I stood outside the elevator for a few minutes, George peeked out of a ladies' room and waved me in.

"You made it!" Bess squealed excitedly, looking up from a diagram she was drawing.

"Of course I did," I confirmed, smiling. "So you guys have had forty minutes—did you case the joint?"

George laughed. "*Did* we!" she said cheerfully. "Nance, the layout here is great for snooping. We were able to get most of the lay of the land by just

discreetly looking into Green Solutions' offices—
their entrance is all glass. From there we could see
the reception area, Cassandra's office, although we
didn't see her, and someone else's—maybe the CFO."

Bess nodded. "But also, there's a window in the
hallway that opens up. By sticking out our heads, we
were able to look into the office next door—which
just happens to be their conference room!" She
grinned. "We've already texted Ned all the details.
The most important thing is that he gets Cassandra
to take him to the conference room—not her office.
That way we can easily search the two offices while
he distracts her down the hall."

I smiled. "See? I knew I was right to leave the
initial snooping in your hands."

Bess laughed, nodding. "I forgot how fun this is,"
she agreed. "Nance, don't take this the wrong way,
but—maybe you should get kidnapped by shady
consultants more often!"

Ned knew better than to look for us when he got
off the elevator an hour or so later. I could tell it
was a struggle for him, but he kept his eyes facing
ahead, and didn't hesitate for a moment before pushing open the door to Green Solutions' offices.

"Hello?" he called.

"Hello?" a pleasant female voice answered. George

and I glanced at each other from our hiding place in a small alcove in the hall that housed a drinking fountain.

"I'm Carson Marvin," Ned announced, impressing me with his smoothness. "We spoke on the phone this morning?"

"Of course, of course," the voice said warmly. I looked at my friends. *That was Cassandra Stevens!* "I've been looking forward to meeting you! Why don't you come into my office?"

*"Actually,"* Ned replied, and I looked nervously at my friends, hoping this little planned switcheroo would work, "do you have a conference room where we could meet? I have several documents to show you that I'd like to . . . spread out. And I have some information on my laptop. Perhaps you have a projector. . . ."

"Oh, sure," Cassandra replied. "That's fine. Let's head to the conference room, then."

I looked at Bess and George. *Success!* Peering around the corner, George glanced back at the two of us before cautiously sneaking down the hallway to peek into the Green Solutions lobby.

"Coast is clear!" she whispered a moment later.

Bess and I looked briefly at each other before stepping into the hallway and following George down to the Green Solutions entrance. With a nervous glance in my direction, George carefully opened the glass door—fortunately the hinges were well-oiled and it didn't make a sound. As quietly as we could, Bess and I slipped through, followed by George.

"Let's start in Cassandra's office," I whispered. "I'd bet she has the biggest secrets to keep."

We tiptoed straight through the lobby and veered to the right to enter Cassandra's huge, bamboo-paneled office. A large window looked out on the lake, and modern, expensive-looking furnishings surrounded a large desk. There was a door in the wall that contained the window, leading, I assumed, to a closet or restroom.

"Okay," Bess whispered. "Same as usual? George takes the computer, I take the filing cabinet, Nance takes the desk?"

"Sounds like a plan," George whispered back, heading right to the computer and grabbing the mouse. I moved behind her to the desk, looking down at the few, neatly-piled papers that were arranged on the edges. Lifting them up, I glanced at each one in turn: office memos, a letter from a satisfied customer, a letter asking for more information . . .

As we searched, I strained my ears to try to hear Ned and Cassandra in the conference room. I couldn't hear anything, which I took as a good sign. Quiet meant a typical, orderly meeting. If Cassandra caught on to Ned's ruse, I was pretty sure there would be raised voices and movement.

After a few minutes, Bess, George, and I fell into our familiar groove. We were silent, knowing that Cassandra might leave the conference room at any moment and hear us. Still, I was so focused on looking at the (so far, completely innocent) papers on Cassandra's desk, I didn't hear Ned until he was just a few feet outside Cassandra's office. . . .

"Oh, this isn't necessary!" he insisted, his voice high and insistent. "I don't need to see the brochure from *inside your office*!"

I looked at my friends. *Oh no!* But Bess and George sprung into action immediately. They both glanced at each other, opened the door next to the window, found a small bathroom, and darted inside. I scrambled to follow them—but just then I glanced down and noticed an interesting piece of paper in one of the open desk drawers. It was handwritten on lined paper, folded into a tight package, and must have been crammed deep enough into the drawer that I'd unearthed it when I'd taken everything else out. I paused, torn. I should really scramble to the restroom—I knew that—but that paper looked *much* more personal and interesting than anything we'd found so far.

I reached out and grabbed it. That's when I heard

Cassandra's voice. "It's right in here. . . ." she was saying right outside the office.

Taking a deep breath, I darted down and under the desk.

Fractions of a second later, I heard two sets of footsteps enter the office.

"Did you hear that?" Cassandra asked.

# NOT-SO-GREEN DIRT

"Hear what?" asked Ned. "In the office, you mean?"

"Yes," said Cassandra, an odd edge to her voice. I pressed my face against the carpet to peer out from the bottom of the desk. I had to struggle to find an angle where I could see both Cassandra and Ned and be fairly sure they couldn't see me, but finally I did. Cassandra looked nothing like the oily, unkempt villain I'd been imagining—she was an attractive, middle-aged redhead, fashionably dressed in eco-friendly-looking fabrics. Both she and Ned had walked about ten feet into the office, and weren't standing far from the front of the desk. They were both facing the desk—and me.

"I didn't hear anything," Ned assured her. "Maybe you have mice."

That's when I saw Bess and George sneak out of the washroom and out the door—Bess casting a regretful look back at the desk, as if to say, *Sorry, Nancy*. I understood, though. When you're snooping and get caught in an uncomfortable situation, you take your opportunities for escape where you can.

Cassandra frowned, looking unconvinced, but she didn't say anything more about the noise. "Well. Let me get what I was going to show you," she said calmly. My heart sped up as she walked around the desk—if she looked underneath, there would be no place for me to hide! There were just a few inches between the bottom of the desk and the rug—not enough space for me to squeeze through. I tried to push myself even deeper into the small wooden cavity as I heard Cassandra's voice come all too close.

"Let me see," she was saying, opening and closing a few desk drawers. "I thought I left it right here. Honestly, I'm such a scatterbrain lately! Could I have dropped it?"

My heart just about stopped. I tried to push back further, expecting Cassandra to drop to her knees and peer under the desk at any moment, but after a few seconds, I heard Cassandra open another drawer and cry, "*There* you are!"

She lifted something up out of the drawer, then walked back over to Ned.

"This is the brochure for the Cartoon Center in Portland. You can see how beautiful and unique it is—and the brochure lists all the ways it's one hundred percent green."

Ned cleared his throat, and there was silence for a moment as he, I assumed, looked at the brochure. "This is very impressive."

Cassandra sounded pleased. "I hoped you'd think so."

Ned sounded hesitant as he went on. "I just wondered—I mean, obviously—you'd propose green ideas as we were planning the building, and we'd approve them."

"That's right," Cassandra agreed. "We provide *green solutions*—just like the name."

Ned coughed. "I just wondered," he went on, "how a client ensured, after the job was done, that all the green fixtures he approved made it into the final product."

I bit my lip. Ned was being gutsy tonight! He was practically asking Cassandra point-blank how what had happened at Casa Verde had happened . . . how Green Solutions allowed a resort to be built with *none* of the green features that Cristobal and Enrique had requested and approved.

There was silence for a moment. "Well," Cassandra

said finally, her voice noticeably less warm than it had been just a moment ago, "I suppose you'd have to ask our hundreds of satisfied customers. I mean . . ." She laughed. "I guess we wouldn't be in business very long if we lied to all of our customers!" She paused again, and her voice, when she spoke again, was almost challenging. "Would we?"

Ned was quiet for a moment, like he was thinking it over. "I suppose not," he said finally.

"Well." Cassandra sounded satisfied now. "I guess we're done here, right? Can I walk you out? I'm finished here for the night, and I just need to lock up."

Ned laughed—nervously, I realized, but I hoped Cassandra wouldn't be able to tell. "Lock up? Sure, I'll wait. Locking up doesn't sound that intense—is it?"

Cassandra laughed, moving behind the desk again. I flinched.

"In most offices, no," she replied, after grabbing something metallic and heavy off a bookshelf. "But we've had several security issues here, and we *do* have priceless trade secrets inside. I'm afraid I've been forced to padlock the door at night."

I jumped a little in my tiny enclosure. *Padlock?* Most office locks allowed you to unlock from within—meaning that it was virtually impossible to get locked inside. With a padlock, though, I knew that would be impossible. I would be spending the night in the Green Solutions offices.

Cassandra still seemed to have her back to Ned, because when I peered out under the desk, he was shooting me a panicked look. I waved to him to go ahead, though. It wouldn't be the first time I'd been locked in an office building overnight—and I hoped to be able to get some more dirt on Green Solutions with no one around.

Cassandra seemed to have gathered her things, and she walked back to Ned. "Shall we?" she asked.

Ned looked nervously back at the desk I hid under— just for a second—then looked up at Cassandra and pasted on a smile. "Sure," he agreed.

I heard them walk out into the lobby, and moments later, they were gone—and from the sound of it, I was padlocked in. I spilled out from beneath the desk, resting on the soft carpet and letting out a long, loud sigh. *Another case, another night trapped in an office building,* I thought resignedly. And I was starving. *I really have to start bringing protein bars when I snoop,* I thought to myself. Still: I had to admit I was a little thrilled at the idea of having twelve hours or so alone in the Green Solutions offices. That was plenty of time to find the evidence I needed—even if it was hidden far from the casual observer's eye.

I settled myself in Cassandra's chair, deciding to start with the obvious. I unfolded the handwritten note I still held, sweat-soaked now, in the palm of my hand. It seemed to be a list of some kind. It was labeled PROJECTS—and, if the Internet research we'd conducted the day before was correct, it seemed to be a list of buildings Green Solutions has consulted on. *Cartoon Building. Meyerhoff Residence. Warhawk Stadium.* Next to each listing was a name and a series of notes: *Recording. Signed contract. E-mails.* These same notes repeated over and over. Looking down, I spotted Enrique's name next to *Casa Verde.* There was a small heart drawn next to his name, and the notes: *Letters. E-mails. Extensive phone recordings.*

I felt my pulse quicken. *Is this a list of dirt Cassandra has on Enrique—and all her clients?*

Just then, I heard a sudden *beep beep beep beep*—a car alarm starting up on the street below. It sounded close—way too close to be coming in through a closed window. I stood and followed the noise. It brought me through the lobby and into a small hallway that led to the conference room—which had a tiny window at its end. I smiled, realizing that the window in the hallway was open. Could it be possible? With all of Cassandra's "security concerns," and that big stupid padlock, someone had forgotten to close a window? I ran over and peered down. Right below

71

me, a system of old metal fire escapes led all the way down, past eight stories, to the ground. Reaching out, I shook the top level—a little rickety, but it looked like it would support my weight. Smiling, I shoved the note I'd found—which I was pretty sure was just the evidence I'd need to catch Cassandra—in my pocket. It looked like I might be heading home with Ned, Bess and George after all!

I pushed the window open enough so that I could squeeze out, then carefully, gingerly, placed my weight on the fire escape. It seemed pretty solid, so I took a deep breath and scrambled down the first flight of stairs to the seventh story. It was a little nerve-racking being so far up—and with so little between me and the cold, hard street—but this wasn't the first time I'd scrambled down a fire escape to freedom.

When I reached the second story, I carefully released the last staircase, pushing it down so it nearly hit the ground. Luckily for me, the fire escape descended into a small alley, so nobody noticed me as I climbed down and let out a little gasp of relief once I reached solid ground. The neighborhood seemed pretty quiet—one of those office-heavy neighborhoods that emptied out after five o'clock. I was glad for that as I slipped out of the alley, unnoticed, and began walking the few blocks to the small park where

Ned, Bess, George, and I had planned to rendezvous after our snooping mission.

The park was tiny, barely more than one building's width, on a quiet corner facing some office buildings. It was pretty, though, with flowering trees and a carefully manicured garden. A few tables and chairs were arranged in an elevated rear area, and I imagined they were probably packed with office workers around lunch hour. I settled on a bench near the street.

My friends were nowhere to be seen.

*Did they leave without me?* I sighed, considering the possibility. When Ned left me in Cassandra's office, it seemed pretty clear that I would be locked in the office overnight. Maybe they had decided it wasn't worth waiting. And with me without my cell, they had no way to contact me. Could I even contact them? I bit my lip, trying to remember their cell phone numbers without my trusty contact list to guide me. I knew I should have them memorized, but . . . hmm . . . Ned's started with a 9, I was pretty sure. . . .

*Rrriiiiiing! Rrriiiiing!*

I jumped at the loud noise, wondering if I had somehow prompted it with my thoughts of phone numbers. My hand automatically reached into my pocket, searching for my cell, but I soon realized it wasn't even my ringtone. It was an old-fashioned ring—like an actual, vibrating bell. And it was coming from . . . behind me.

*Rrrrriiiing! Rrrriiiiing!*

It was coming from a pay phone in the elevated area with the tables and chairs.

I frowned. It sure was loud, and as I watched it, it rang another three . . . four . . . five times. I hadn't even known pay phones could get incoming calls, but I supposed it was possible on some older models. One thing was for sure: Whoever was on the other end of the line wasn't giving up. It had to be a wrong number. Sighing, trying to block the sound from my mind, I searched the street for my friends.

There was no one around, though. The streets were desolate and creepily silent—which only made the ringing stand out more. I shifted on the bench, agitated. It had to have rung . . . fifteen, sixteen times now?

*Hang up!* I screamed in my mind, wishing the noise would cease. *Wrong number! Try again!*

Suddenly, after one more ring, there was silence. I let out the breath I hadn't even realized I was holding. *There. That's better.* I looked around. Five more minutes? Maybe if I waited that long, and my friends didn't come, I could call my father on the pay phone and have him call Ned and ask him to double back . . . if I could find a quarter, that was . . . I was always—

*Rrrrriiiiing! Rrrrrrriiiing!*

I froze in my seat. The ringing continued again, on and on, long after any normal caller would have given up. I shivered, suddenly feeling uncomfortable. It was getting dark, and with the darkness came a cold wind off the lake. I was pretty sure my friends had left me, and I was alone in a deserted area of the big city.

*Rrrriiiiing! Rrrriiiing!*

*And that phone wouldn't stop ringing!*

Hugging my sides, I got up and ran to the phone. I could at least tell this person it was a wrong number—he or she was calling a pay phone in some deserted park. Then I could call my father and arrange a meeting point for Ned to pick me up.

"Hello?" I said, grabbing the receiver. "Listen, you have the wrong—"

But a voice cut me off. A robotic, distorted voice—the voice I'd heard on the other end of my cell phone this morning. "Hello, Nancy. We see you've been distracting yourself in the big city on silly errands. Did you find anything useful?"

My blood froze. *How could they—?*

Laughter filled the line—cold, robotic laughter. "I thought not. While you've been out of town, we

75

visited your house. And we have someone with us you might recognize."

My mouth dropped open, but I couldn't make a sound. *This can't be real. This can't be happening. How could they—?*

I heard the phone being handed over, and then a familiar voice: "Nancy? Nancy, are you—?"

My heart squeezed. I dropped the phone.

*They had Hannah!*

# 8

# UNEXPECTED CALLS

I stood facing the pay phone, my mouth wide open, my heart racing. Whoever was on the other end of that line . . . whoever was behind that cold, robotic voice . . . they had gotten into my house. They had taken Hannah, the person who's the closest thing to a mother that I've had since my own mother passed away. I felt my stomach twist, and wondered if I was going to throw up.

*Don't hurt her!* I wanted to scream. *Don't you dare even touch her!*

That's when I realized I'd dropped the phone, and in doing so, had possibly cut the only connection I had with Hannah's abductors. Suddenly panicked, I grabbed the phone and held the receiver to my ear.

"Hello? Hello? Are you still there?"

But all I heard was the *beep beep beep* of a dead line. Hannah's abductors had hung up.

Placing the phone back in its cradle, I took a deep breath. My heart was racing, and I could feel adrenaline running through my veins, making me want to run, fight, scream—anything but sit here on this stupid pay phone. But I also knew I couldn't handle this alone. Digging desperately for all the change in my pocket, I dialed one number I knew by heart: the River Heights Police Department.

"River Heights PD."

"Hi," I said quickly, "this is Nancy Drew. Is Officer Yang available?"

"Hold on."

There was a pause of a minute or so before Officer Yang picked up the phone. "Miss Drew, let me tell you, you have some nerve—"

I swallowed. *Oh, right.* The last time I'd seen Officer Yang, I'd kind of been ditching him in a fake popcorn-fueled catastrophe.

"I know," I said quickly, cutting him off. "I don't have time to get into detail here, Officer Yang, but truly: I had no other choice, and I meant no disrespect. But something has happened and I desperately, desperately need your help."

There was another pause, and then Officer Yang snorted. "Have you been kidnapped again?"

"No." As briefly as I could, I explained to Officer Yang what had happened. He perked up when I got to the part about the stranger putting Hannah on the phone.

"You're sure it was her?"

"Positive," I replied, without hesitation. I'd know her voice anywhere. She'd practically raised me. "Listen, I know you don't completely believe that I was kidnapped yesterday or that Green Solutions is involved, but I really need you to check out their River Heights warehouse and see if Hannah is there."

Officer Yang asked me for a few more details, but soon promised that he and his partner were getting into their car now. "We'll check it out immediately."

"Thank you, Officer Yang. And, really—I'm sorry for ditching you."

He didn't reply, but after a moment, promised: "I'll be in touch soon." I gave him the pay phone number, then hung up.

My next call was to my father. I wasn't sure what I expected. If whoever had Hannah had taken her from the house, I realized, there was a chance my father was in danger too. The police "protectors" had followed me to the university this afternoon— leaving the house completely vulnerable. Now, when

I thought about it, that seemed really shortsighted of me. If Cassandra wanted to hurt me, what would stop her from hurting my family? From hurting *anybody* I cared about in an effort to get to me?

My home phone rang and rang, but nobody picked up. Finally the answering machine kicked in; my father's deep voice, saying, "The Drews are not in right now. Please leave a message . . ."

I swallowed. *Oh, gosh, Dad, please be all right.* "Dad," I said at the beep. "This is *very important.* If you get this, call me right away at . . ." I left the pay phone's number.

After that, I called his office number, but there was no answer there, either. I closed my eyes, praying silently to myself: *Please don't have Dad. Please don't have Dad. Please let Hannah be okay. . . .*

*Rrrrriiiiing!* I jumped at the sudden loud noise, then grabbed the pay phone receiver.

"Hello?"

"Nancy? This is Officer Yang."

My breath caught. "And?" I managed to choke out.

"We're at the warehouse now. There doesn't seem to be anyone here—and there's no sign anyone's been here today."

I let out my breath, feeling like I was deflating.

"Thank you," I managed finally, "for checking it out."

"Of course," Officer Yang replied, his voice warming with sympathy. "And of course we'll continue to check this out. We'll go by your house now."

"Thanks."

We spoke a bit more—Officer Yang asking for a few details of the call he hadn't had time for during our first conversation—then we said our good-byes. Hanging up, I sighed, staring at the phone. I fished out another thirty-five cents and dialed home again—still no answer.

I looked around, trying to calm myself down. It was getting really dark now. It looked like Bess, George, and Ned assumed I was stuck and didn't wait. Our snooping didn't really reveal anything about Green Solutions—just some cryptic notes I wasn't totally sure meant anything. And now Cassandra—I *knew* it must be Cassandra—had Hannah, and possibly my dad.

Suddenly remembering, I fished in my wallet and found an international calling card I'd bought in Costa Rica. I'd used it to call Ned a couple times, and my dad once—and I was pretty sure it had an hour or so left on it.

I picked up the phone and dialed. There's only one person who could help me right now, by telling me the truth. *"Hola?"*

"Hello, Juliana," I said. "I need to speak to your father. I'm desperate."

Juliana was quiet for a moment. "Nancy?" she asked finally, hesitantly. "Did you get to Cassandra? Have you proven anything?"

I sighed. How I wished I could tell her "yes"! "I'm trying," I replied. "Look, Juliana, I don't have a lot of time. I'm calling you from a pay phone in Chicago. I'm trying my best to get dirt on Cassandra, but it's difficult. She has some very scary people working for her. They've attacked my family and they're holding"—my voice broke—"they're holding Hannah, who practically raised me. Listen to me, Juliana. I *need* to talk to your father. My only hope of getting out of this is his telling me the truth about Green Solutions."

A few seconds passed before Juliana replied. "Wow. I'm sorry, Nancy, but—"

"But what?" I snapped, getting impatient. "Are you at the hospital? Juliana, please help me."

"I am," Juliana admitted. "And in fact, he's right here. But he won't talk to you, Nancy. He won't talk to anyone."

I took a deep breath. "Put him on the line," I instructed in a voice that invited no dissent.

"But—"

"*Put him on the line,*" I repeated, and then softened my voice. "Please, Juliana."

I heard her sigh. "Okay," she said finally. There was quiet for a moment as the phone shifted, and then I heard Juliana's voice explaining to her father in Spanish. The only words I could make out were *Nancy Drew.*

Finally I heard breathing, and knew the phone had been put to Enrique's ear. "Enrique," I began, "I know you're not feeling well, but listen. I need your help. My family is in danger, Enrique. When I came home to Chicago, I tried to get information about Green Solutions, but they're on to me. They're willing to do anything to get me to stop. I believe they tried to kidnap me, and right now they're holding Hannah, who is like family to me." I paused. "Enrique, they're doing this to frighten me, to make me stop investigating them. I believe this is because they cheat their clients. They promise to use eco-friendly fixtures and plans, but they switch them out at the last minute. Maybe the clients know about it, maybe they don't. But in every case, they're scared to speak up."

I heard Enrique sigh and clear his throat. That was good! Maybe I was close to convincing him to tell me the truth. . . .

"Please, Enrique," I went on. "Look, we already know you were involved in the un-green building. You've taken the blame completely on yourself, and I think that's because you're afraid to speak up about Cassandra. And maybe you're feeling guilty, too— guilty about what happened to Sara over the last week."

Another sigh.

"The thing is," I went on, "the only way to stop Cassandra from hurting more people is to tell the truth. Until you do, she's going to keep hurting people. Enrique, she could be hurting Hannah right now." I paused to swipe the back of my hand over my eye—I could feel tears welling up. "And Enrique—I won't stop looking until I have the truth. That means Cassandra won't stop coming after me. You can save me a lot of steps, Enrique. Please, please, just tell me the truth." I paused, my voice breaking again. "Please."

There was silence for a moment. I could hear Enrique taking in a breath, and my heart pounded. Was he going to tell me? Had I convinced him? Could this really be the end of it?

But then I heard a sound like someone throwing something, and a loud *clank* as the receiver hit the floor. I could hear Enrique in the background, shouting, *"No! No! No!"*

My heart sank. He sounded really upset—and not totally rational. I had gotten to him with what I'd said. But not the right way. Not in a way that would make him confess.

After a moment, Juliana came back on the line. "I'm sorry, Nancy," she said, sounding sincere, "but as you can hear, my father is not in a good way. I have to go."

The line clicked off before I could answer.

I closed my eyes, trying to compose myself. *I will not cry. I will fix this. I will not cry.*

The truth, though, was that I didn't know what to do. I desperately wanted to get back to River Heights, try to find my father, and to look for Hannah. But I also knew that until I had some evidence against Green Solutions, we would all still be in danger. Maybe we'd be lucky and the police would find Hannah, or they'd agree to watch our house for another day or two. But then that would be over, and we'd still be in danger. Cassandra was never going to give up trying to stop me from finding the truth. That much was clear now.

And I owed it to Juliana and Enrique and the countless potential victims Cassandra was wooing right now to find the truth.

I looked down at the list in my hand, the list I stole from Cassandra's office. I couldn't help but believe it was the key—if not to the whole case, then at least to *something*.

I cleared my throat, trying to pull myself together. Then, hardly believing I was doing it, I dug in my wallet for a business card and dialed the number.

It was picked up on the first ring. "Hello? *New York Globe.*"

I sighed. "Hello, Frankie? I need your help."

# 9

## AN UNLIKELY ALLY

"Hi, Frankie," I said quietly, fiddling with the phone cord. "It's me, Nancy Drew." "Nancy?" Frankie asked. She didn't sound exactly excited to hear from me ... but then she didn't sound disgusted, either. Frankie and I had an odd relationship in Costa Rica: part partners-in-crime, part competitors. Frankie could be a little arrogant and aggressive in her questioning. During the brief part of my vacation when I'd teamed up with her to get to the bottom of Casa Verde's troubles, I hadn't quite trusted her. Still . . . I had to admit, she seemed like a heck of an investigative reporter. And she was the only person I could think of who might have the information I desperately needed right now.

"Is this a bad time?" I asked. "I kind of . . . need your help."

Frankie was silent for a moment. I felt certain she was wondering what type of help I might be asking for. "It's a fine time," she said finally. "I'm still at work, actually."

"*Still?*" I asked. It was almost nine in Chicago . . . in New York it would be even later. I knew Frankie was a workaholic, but that seemed awfully late to be at your desk.

"I know." Frankie let out a sigh that sounded like equal parts *Oh, poor me!* and *Isn't it great?* "I'm working on this huge story right now. It's about a scandal in the New York City subway, where they might have diverted . . . oh, never mind. It's complicated, I don't want to confuse you. Anyway, I'm waiting for a couple people to call me back, so I figured I'd hang around." She paused. "Anyway?" She asked finally. "You needed . . .?"

"I'm sorry," I said, "I guess I just . . . need a fellow investigative mind."

I could practically hear Frankie's smile over the phone. "I like the sound of that," she replied. "What can I help you with?"

Briefly, I caught her up on everything that had happened to me since Bess, George, and I returned from Casa Verde. The car service . . . the kidnapping attempt . . . what I'd learned from Cristobal . . . and my promise to Juliana. Then I explained our trip today, my snooping escapade in Green Solutions' offices, and the call to the pay phone. When I got to the part about Hannah and my father, Frankie gasped.

"Nancy," she said in a grave voice, "this sounds serious. Do you know how much danger you could be in?"

I sighed. "I do," I admitted, "but I'm more worried about Dad and Hannah right now. Frankie, I need to get to them. I need to get Hannah away from these guys. They tried to kill me, more than once— who knows what they might be willing to do to my family?"

Frankie was silent for a moment, thinking that over. When she spoke, it was in a low voice. "You're very brave, Nancy. I give you credit for that."

I wasn't sure what to say to that. "Thanks." I swallowed, looking down at the list in my hands. "Frankie, I told you about the piece of paper I grabbed from Cassandra's desk—the list of names and different types of information."

"Right," Frankie responded quickly. "You said it looked like a list of dirt Cassandra has on these people."

"Exactly," I replied. "I wondered—if I read you

some of the names, maybe you could look them up for me? You must have access to a news search engine."

Again, I felt like I could hear Frankie's smile. "But of course," she replied. "Let me just bring it up on my computer. . . . There we go. Okay, Nancy, read away."

I read off the names in sequence, and I could hear Frankie typing them into her search engine. "Nothing" she said about Gavin Dunmar; "Nada" about Orren Kilkowski; and "Squat" about Sylvia Davies. I sighed, wondering if we were heading down the wrong path.

"Joe Lentrichia," I read, waiting for Frankie's negative response.

Instead she replied, "Bingo." I heard furious typing and clicking as Frankie sifted through the search contents.

"Lots of articles about this one," Frankie explained, "all in your town of Chicago. Seems Mr. Lentrichia is the owner of Joey's Deep Dish—a pizza chain I guess is big over there?"

"I've heard of it," I replied, tightly. In fact, I was pretty sure Ned and I had shared a pie at one of their locations once.

"Anyway," Frankie went on, "it seems Mr. Lentrichia consulted with Green Solutions to build a huge, eco-friendly, mega restaurant on Wacker

Drive." She paused. "You know where that is?"

"Vaguely," I admitted. Chicago geography is not my strong point, but I thought it was west of where I was.

"It seems," Frankie went on, "that when the mega restaurant opened, Mr. Lentrichia ended up on the news at the center of a big scandal. His supposedly green restaurant turned out to be anything but. In fact, his supposedly green pizza ovens were releasing noxious chemicals into the air—damaging the ozone layer, and putting all of his neighbors' health at risk."

I thought that over. Come to think of it, had I seen something about that in the news? A pizza mogul dethroned . . . "Wow," I breathed. "I think I remember something about that. But the restaurant is still open . . . ?"

"Right," Frankie confirmed. "And what's interesting is, Joe never turned around and blamed Green Solutions—even though he consulted with them on that very subject, how to create a totally green restaurant, and even though they signed off on his designs. Instead, he spent an estimated two *million* dollars to fix the problem himself." She paused. "Pretty weird behavior for a businessman, no? He could have sued Cassandra and probably gotten enough to fix the problem."

I frowned, thinking about it. "It's not weird," I

replied, glancing at my list, "if she has 'recordings and e-mails' that he wouldn't want released. Recordings, say, of him agreeing to scrap some green initiatives to save some cash, or e-mails where he agrees to some shady building ideas."

Frankie chuckled. "Exactly, Miss Drew," she said, and I heard her clicking around on the news story. "I think Mr. Joe Lentrichia, of 45 Maple Avenue, might have a story to tell us about Green Solutions."

My heart was pounding. "I have to go talk to him," I said, looking around the park for a taxi or el station. "Forty-five Maple, you said, right? I don't think that's far. . . ."

Frankie's voice changed abruptly, all the laughter and levity suddenly gone. "Nancy . . . I don't think that's a good idea. . . ."

"You don't understand," I insisted, still searching for a cab. "They have *Hannah*, Frankie. They might have my father. I have to find out the real story!"

Frankie tried on a soothing tone. "I know, Nancy, I understand you're scared, but . . . don't you think this is a little rash?"

"Rash?" I asked, scoffing. "It was *rash* of Cassandra to take Hannah. It was *rash* of her to try to kill me."

"I just don't want you to put yourself in danger, Nancy," Frankie went on, sounding honestly concerned now. "Couldn't you wait for the police?"

"The police won't question him immediately," I replied, "and you know it. Come on, Frankie, you know nobody cares about this case as much as I do."

Frankie was quiet for a moment. "Nancy," she said finally. "I know you think you're invincible, but you're not. None of us are. Just wait for—"

That's when I spotted it: a yellow cab about a block away.

"I have to go, Frankie. There's a cab." I shoved the phone back into place, hearing Frankie's cries of protest until the connection was severed. Then I shoved my hand in my pocket, pulled out my wallet, and began running after the taxi.

Joe Lentrichia was about to have an unexpected visitor.

# A DESPERATE PLEA

The taxi driver drove me into a bright, fashionable part of the city. Expensive boutiques lined the streets, and well-dressed people filled fancy-looking restaurants with tables spilling out onto the sidewalk. I looked around, trying to figure out whether Joe Lentrichia might be among them, or where he might live.

"Here we go, Miss," announced the driver, pulling to a stop in front of a French bistro. "Forty-five Maple Avenue."

I looked around, momentarily confused. Joe Lentrichia lived in a restaurant? But then I saw a doorway off to the side labeled 45 and presumably leading up to apartments above. I thanked the driver, paid him with some of the last bills in my wallet, and climbed out.

I was nervous. I had no idea what kind of person Joe Lentrichia might be; I worried that he would be just as bad as Cassandra, willing to do whatever was necessary to get rid of me. But I hoped he would hear me out and feel some sympathy for my plight once I told him what Cassandra had done to me. Maybe she had put him in a similar situation. After all, I couldn't imagine any businessman paying millions to fix a problem that wasn't his fault without a good reason.

I entered the doorway marked 45 and walked inside the small, but well-lit and luxuriously furnished, foyer. A line of intercom buzzers was on the wall to my right. I looked, and found a buzzer marked LENTRICHIA—Apartment 4. Taking a deep breath, I pressed it.

"Yeah?" asked a gruff voice after just a few seconds.

"Flower delivery for you," I blurted, forcing the words out. I like to use "flower delivery" because nobody knows when they're getting flowers, and most are willing to entertain the idea. Based on Joe Lentrichia's reaction, though, I didn't think he was entirely convinced.

"What?" he asked, sounding confused. "Who sent me flowers?"

*Ummmmm . . .*

"I'm not sure," I replied. "I don't have the card handy and, Sir, it's eight dozen roses. I can't really reach the purchase order right now. May I bring them up?"

"Someone sent me eight dozen roses?" He sounded only half-convinced.

I took a deep breath. "That's right, Sir. You must have a very enthusiastic secret admirer."

There was no response for a moment, then a buzzer sounded—I was being buzzed into the building! "Come on up," he said, still not sounding terribly excited. But I didn't care. I was in! I ran over to the glass door that led to the apartments, threw it open, and darted in.

There was an elevator to the left, and that seemed to be the only way to reach the apartments. I had a feeling these might be old industrial loft apartments—entire floors made into apartments. This feeling was backed up when the elevator came and each floor was labeled with a name—2, CONNOR. 3, MOREAU. 4, LENTRICHIA.

I pressed 4 and waited. Slowly, the old elevator lifted into service, and I could feel myself rising slowly. I tried to use breathing to calm myself down. *It will be okay. . . . He'll listen to me. . . .*

*Thunk!* The elevator stopped abruptly, apparently on the fourth floor.

As the doors opened, I saw that I was right: The room that I faced was huge, surrounded by enormous, floor-to-ceiling windows, with high ceilings. A small kitchen area stood off to my right, with glass cabinets, a sink, and a huge, expensive-looking stovetop and oven. Straight ahead was a large living area: plush-looking blue carpet, a brown leather sofa, and two cushy, oversize ivory chairs.

Sitting in one of those chairs, facing me, was the man I assumed to be Joe Lentrichia. He was a relatively young guy—maybe in his thirties?—with dark eyes, dark, close-cropped hair, and a wiry build. He was wearing dark jeans with an orange T-shirt and a gray blazer. He was talking on the phone, but he watched me curiously as I entered his apartment. The elevator doors closed behind me, and I could hear the ancient machine heading back to the ground floor.

"Yeah," he was saying to whoever was on the other end of the line, "it seems like exactly what you expected. Okay."

He abruptly pulled the cell phone from his ear and hung up, frowning at me. "Where are my roses?" he asked, sounding unamused. "I was told I had a secret admirer."

I moved closer to him, trying to look as desperate as I felt. "Please," I said. "Just hear me out. The truth is I don't have any flowers for you. The truth is . . . I need your help."

He looked at me skeptically. "What could you need my help for?" he asked. "You look all of, what . . . fourteen?"

I sighed. "It doesn't matter how old I am," I insisted, which was the truth. "What matters is that I think we're both in the same boat. We're both being threatened and harassed by Cassandra Samuels."

That seemed to get through to him. His eyes widened. "What do you know about Cassandra?" he asked.

I moved a little closer. We were now standing just about ten feet apart. "I don't *know*," I said, "but I'm pretty sure she swindles people for a living. She gets them to pay her big bucks to design an eco-friendly building for them, then at the last minute, switches all the green features out for cheap, shoddy materials. I think that's what happened to you," I went on, giving him a meaningful look. "I think you got in trouble about your restaurant because Cassandra tricked you. She installed those cheap ovens after telling you she'd use green fixtures. Isn't that right?"

Joe didn't say anything, but something dark seemed to flash across his eyes. "Easy, there," he said, lowering his voice.

"But it doesn't end there," I went on, trying to catch his eye. "I think Cassandra has something on you. Something she knows you don't want to get out. Either you approved the cheap fixtures, or she caught you doing or saying something else that could get you into trouble. It's bad enough that you were willing to pay millions to fix the problems in your restaurants yourself, rather than hold Cassandra accountable."

Joe was looking me in the eye now. "You should leave," he said, but he didn't move from the chair.

"Joe," I said, still hoping that what I was saying was penetrating. "Listen. I've gotten myself in a lot of trouble, and I think you can help me get out of it. A little over a week ago, I started investigating Cassandra and Green Solutions. She found out somehow, and now she wants me gone. She tried to *kidnap* me, Joe. She brought me out to a warehouse in the middle of nowhere and . . ." I shuddered. "I don't even know, Joe, what she would have done to me if I hadn't escaped."

Joe looked me in the eye, then away. He seemed to be thinking this over. "So?" he asked finally. "What does this have to do with me?"

I breathed in. I was getting to him! "She has a member of my family," I said. "Right now. I don't know what she'll do to her. Listen, Joe, I need your help to take Cassandra down. We both know she's dangerous. But I don't have any proof—you do. You *must*. If you tell the truth about what Cassandra did to you—why you were willing to pay millions to avoid shining a light on her—the police will listen to you, they'll take you seriously. Together we can make sure she never hurts anyone else!"

Joe sighed, ran his hands through his hair, and looked down at his lap. "Little girl," he said after a few seconds. "I can't help you. If you want to stay out of trouble, you should leave now."

I shook my head. Didn't he understand me? "I *can't* leave," I insisted. "Didn't you hear me? My safety is at stake, Joe. And my family member—" My voice cracked then. *Darn it!* Why was it so hard to convince the people Cassandra had swindled to help me? What did she have on them? "She could be hurting her right now. . . ."

I felt tears welling up in my eyes, and again wiped them away with the back of my hand.

Joe was watching me, silent. His eyes looked sympathetic.

"Please," I begged. "Help me save her! Help me stop Cassandra. . . ."

Joe shook his head, slowly. "Little girl . . ."

I coughed, choking on my tears. "I'm not a *little girl*," I insisted, "I'm Nancy Drew. Don't you understand me? Do you know the kind of people you're dealing with here? People willing to kidnap, maim, even kill?"

I looked him in the eye. He opened his mouth again, but said nothing.

"She tried to kill me," I went on, "more than once. And that was before I even came close to realizing how dangerous she was. Do you—?"

That's when I heard the elevator. I heard it creaking into place before the bell rang and the doors opened. Immediately, footsteps thunked into the apartment behind me, followed by voices:

"All right, Nancy Drew, just turn around slowly, no funny stuff. You're coming with us!"

I closed my eyes, feeling a tear leak out and slide down the side of my nose. When I opened them, Joe Lentrichia was looking at me with deep regret. *I'm sorry,* he mouthed as a short, muscular man grabbed me from behind and another man—taller, wearing sunglasses even though it was dark outside—roughly took hold of my shoulder. A third man, who was bald, circled around to face me.

"You should've known better, Missy," he said, smiling meanly. "Coming right into the home of one of Cassandra's clients? You think she wasn't watching them?"

I swallowed hard. What was it Joe had said into the phone when I arrived? *It seems like exactly what you expected.*

He'd been talking to Cassandra.

About me.

I didn't put up much of a fight as the shortest man fished the handwritten list out of my pocket and shoved it into his jeans. Together, the three men grabbed me by the arms and shoulders, making it impossible for me to twist away.

"You're coming with us," the sunglasses-wearing man told me with a cruel smile. "Betcha can't guess where."

I couldn't. But I knew what would happen to me once I got there: I would be silenced. One way or another. And somewhere else, someone might be doing the same to Hannah.

I felt a sob growing in my throat.

"Come on," the short man said roughly, yanking me toward the elevator. The other two followed. I tried to put up a fight—to buck, twist, or duck away—but it was impossible. These men were obviously experienced in taking people against their will.

I glanced back at Joe Lentrichia, who was watching

this whole show with a stricken expression, like he couldn't believe his own part in it. He caught my eye and shook his head, but I looked away. I didn't care about his regret.

I'd failed.

And now who knew what was going to happen to me?

The elevator seemed to take forever to get to the ground floor, and right before the doors opened, the short man got up in my face.

"We're going out to my car," he snarled at me. "If you so much as make a peep—if you try to attract any attention—you will pay for it later. Understand?"

I nodded, unsure what to do. Making a scene might be my only hope . . . but what if nobody noticed? What if it backfired?

Slowly, the men led me out of the foyer and into the brightly lit street. A dark car was waiting right at the curb. Summoning all the courage I had, I took a deep breath, ready to let out the loudest scream of my entire life. But before I could get enough air—

Flashbulbs. They were exploding all around us!

I squinted in the direction they came from, but spots were swimming in front of my eyes—I couldn't make out anything. Then I heard a familiar voice.

"Smile, gentlemen!" It was Hildy Kent, freelance writer and one of the friends I'd made in Costa Rica. "You want to look good for the front page of the *New York Globe*!"

# HOME AGAIN, HOME AGAIN . . .

Faced with a barrage of flashbulbs, the three men who were holding me panicked and loosened their grip. That was all I needed to wrench myself away, lifting my elbow to hit the bald man in the face as I pulled back, hard, knocking one of the others off balance. Then I ran as fast as I could over to Hildy, trying to show her in my eyes how incredibly grateful I was.

"Get in the car, Nancy," she said forcefully, gesturing to the black coupe behind her. "I'll take you home."

I let out a sigh of relief, grabbing the passenger side door and lowering myself in. Still taking pictures,

Hildy backed away, opened the door on the other side, and slowly dropped into the driver's seat. "They're running away," Hildy told me, watching the street. I couldn't even bring myself to look at them. "Cowards, just like I thought. They know we know who they're working for and don't want to be caught on camera."

With that, she turned the key in the ignition and put the car in drive.

It took me a few seconds to get myself together enough to turn to her and say, "Hildy . . . I can't thank you enough. You might have saved my life back there."

Driving the car toward the highway now, she shot me a sideways glance. "It was a gutsy move confronting that guy, Nance," she said, shaking her head. "Stupid, but gutsy. You're a firecracker, all right. If I were your mother, I don't think I'd sleep much."

I laughed. "Well, my dad is used to it," I admitted.

"Does he know you were here?"

I looked at her like she was crazy. "No," I said, but then realized: "But I don't know where he is either. Please Hildy—we have to hurry home. I think someone may have broken into my house."

Hildy nodded, shooting me a sympathetic look. "Frankie called me and told me everything. Believe me, I'm putting pedal to the metal to get us there ASAP. But, Nancy, you hung up on Frankie before she could tell you that Joe Lentrichia is widely believed to be an accomplice to Green Solutions, not their victim. Many believe he made a deal with Cassandra to share the money they'd save from using subpar fixtures and de-greening his restaurant. That's why he wouldn't shift the blame to her, even as he was getting in serious trouble."

I nodded. "I think he was on the phone with her when I showed up."

Hildy looked serious. "They must have been thinking you might pay him a visit."

I closed my eyes, rubbing my temples and trying to take this all in. "Are they *watching* me? Did Cassandra leave out the note that led me to him on purpose? Hildy, I'm so confused. I haven't been involved in anything *this* big or *this* scary for a long time."

Hildy nodded, her eyes warm. "I'm not sure what to make of it myself," she admitted, "but there's something much bigger going on here than just what happened at Casa Verde. I don't think Cassandra is your run-of-the-mill greedy businesswoman gone bad. I think from now on, Nancy, you have to be very careful. . . . Don't go in there alone."

I took a deep breath, remembering the feeling of

those three men holding me, and being unable to break away. Where would they have taken me? Had they done the same to Hannah? I shuddered.

This was getting *seriously* scary.

It probably wasn't long, but it felt like forever before we took the exit for River Heights and drove down the streets that led to our house. My breath caught when I saw lights on inside; did that mean my father was home? That he, at least, was safe and could help me find Hannah?

When Hildy stopped the car, I had already unbuckled my seatbelt. I vaulted out of the car toward the house. With Hildy trailing behind, I ran up to the front door, found it unlocked, and threw it open.

"DAD?" I screamed, looking to the right, to the left, and up the stairs. "DAD, ARE YOU HERE?"

Immediately, I heard footfalls approaching from the kitchen. I looked up to see my friends: Bess, George, Ned. And right behind them—looking hugely relieved himself—my dad.

I almost fainted from relief.

The one person I wanted to see more than any-thing—Hannah—wasn't at the house. That didn't sur-prise me, but it still disappointed me. A few minutes later, the rest of us—Bess, George, Ned, Hildy, my dad, and me—settled in our living room to catch up. Bess and George were happy to see Hildy again—we'd all gotten along well on our Casa Verde "vacation"—but clearly curious to learn how we'd ended up together tonight.

"Nancy, I have some very upsetting news," my father said, looking unsure how to relay it. George, Bess, and Ned were all looking at me sympatheti- cally.

"I know about Hannah," I said simply. "In fact, finding out about her was a big part of what hap- pened to me tonight. . . ."

Though I knew it would upset my dad, I went on to tell them everything that had happened since they'd left me in Cassandra's office. With Hannah's safety hanging in the balance, I knew I had to come totally clean about what I knew. My friends' eyes widened when I got to the part about going to Joe Lentrichia's loft, and Ned cried, "Nance! What were you thinking?" My dad just watched me, not saying anything—but I could see the worry in his eyes.

"I was thinking that I had to save her," I replied, shaking my head at my own foolishness. "I was think- ing that Joe Lentrichia might be my only chance to get the truth about Cassandra and Green Solutions. Until I have that, no one will take me seriously about how big a threat she is, and we'll all be in danger from her again soon."

I looked around; everyone seemed to be unhappily in agreement. Still, I could see they weren't thrilled that I'd tried to confront Joe alone.

"Anyway," I went on, "thank goodness Frankie called Hildy right after she talked to me, because she sprung into action and really saved me from who knows what." I went on to explain what had happened at Joe's apartment: trying to convince him, and then being attacked by the three goons.

"Cassandra sent them," I explained. "I'm sure of it. I think he was on the phone with her when I walked in."

Hildy nodded. "He and Cassandra are thought to be in cahoots," she said to my dad and my friends. "Business partners, in a way. I agree that what almost happened to Nancy has Cassandra written all over it."

Ned shook his head, looking stunned. "She seemed so normal in our meeting," he said in amazement. Ned, Bess, and George had already filled my father in on our little snooping trip to Chicago earlier that day.

My father frowned. "Not every crook looks like a lowlife, Ned," he said, shaking his head. "Which is why the sort of things you did today are incredibly dangerous, Nancy. I understand why you felt you had to do them, but still—I wish you'd told me all of this earlier. We could have worked on a solution together."

I nodded, glancing down at my lap. He was right; I'd behaved recklessly. "I'm sorry, Dad."

He nodded, still frowning. "Well," he said finally. "We're not going to get anywhere by focusing on the past. What concerns me right now is Hannah. When I came home from a quick trip to the library this afternoon, she was gone—and there were some broken glasses in the kitchen, signs of a struggle. At first I thought we'd been victims of a robbery. But when I looked around, I was shocked to find this on the refrigerator." He picked up a piece of paper from the coffee table and handed it to me. It was a note, written on a computer.

STOP WHAT YOU'RE DOING. STOP
SNOOPING. STOP POKING YOUR
NOSE WHERE IT'S NOT WANTED
OR MANY PEOPLE YOU LOVE WILL
SUFFER. STARTING WITH THIS ONE.

I swallowed hard, almost unable to believe it. Someone had really broken into our home. Someone had really taken Hannah! My eyes flooded with tears as I asked myself, *Where is she right now? Is she scared? Are they hurting her?*

I felt tears welling in my eyes, and soon I was crying. My father stood up and came over to hug me, patting my back.

"Try to calm down, Nancy. I know this is hard, but we have to stay focused if we want to find Hannah."

I sniffled. "Did they dust the note for fingerprints?" I asked. (Even in my most emotional moments, I have trouble turning off the detective gene sometimes.)

My father nodded, smiling sadly. "They did, Nance. Good call. But they found nothing. Whoever did this—they're not amateurs. They know what they're doing. Oh—and there's something else."

I looked up, amazed that it could get any worse. "There is? What?"

My father looked serious. "Nancy, Cassandra Samuels is missing. Police went to question her but found no sign of her at her condo, and her car was gone from the parking garage."

I groaned, sniffling again and putting my head in my hands. "She took off! She knows we're on to her! Who would have thought that an environmental consulting firm could be a huge criminal conspiracy?"

I asked. Wiping my eyes, I turned to Hildy, Bess, and George. "Remember when we thought we were going to have a super relaxing vacation in Costa Rica?"

My friends smiled sadly. Bess moved over to pat my shoulder. "We'll get through it, Nance," she promised.

"Yeah," agreed George, plopping herself next to me on the other side. "You've taken on scary criminal conspiracies before. We'll come out on top, trust me."

I sighed, wiping at my eyes again. "But I got nothing today," I said, holding back another sob. "After all that, I got nothing."

My father stood up then, glancing at his watch. "Kids," he said in a serious voice, then, with a smile, he glanced at Hildy, "Everyone . . . it's past one o'clock in the morning. I know the police are working hard to find Hannah and will alert us the moment they find anything. Right now, I think the best thing we can do for her is get some sleep so we can get a running start tomorrow. First thing, Nancy, we'll investigate any property Cassandra or Green Solutions owns . . . anywhere they might have taken her." He paused. "But I need access to official records to do that, and I can't get that until business hours start tomorrow. So for now . . ."

Bess nodded, yawning. "I guess we could all use some rest."

I looked at Hildy. "Hildy, you can go home if you want. I'm sure Robin is waiting for you." Hildy had an adorable eight-year-old daughter who'd accompanied us on the Green Solutions trip. But now, she shook her head.

"Robin is safe with her grandparents, who are no doubt spoiling her rotten," she said with a smile. "I'll stay, if it's all right with you. I was at Casa Verde too . . . and I want to get to the bottom of this."

"Okay." I nodded and smiled. "I guess we'd better start taking dibs on the couches, then."

In the end, we were all too freaked out to sleep alone, so we ended up just kind of grabbing a spot wherever we could in the living room. My dad slept next door on the couch in his office. Pretty soon, a chorus of snores and sleepy sighs could be heard all around me. I was pretty sure I was the last one awake.

I was exhausted, but my mind was racing too fast to get to sleep. Images paraded through my brain: Joe Lentrichia in his loft, Cassandra in her office, the fire escape leading down to the alley, the creepy park and the sound of that phone ringing. And then, finally,

Hannah. Where was she tonight? Was she able to get any sleep? Was she in pain?

Hours passed; I watched the time tick by on the mantle clock. One o'clock, then two o'clock, then two thirty. That was the last time I remember. One minute, it was silent and dark and I was wide awake; the next, I was awaking from a deep sleep, and somebody was pounding on the door. Pale light shone in through the windows: It had to be around 6 a.m.

My father stumbled into the living room from the den. "Who could that be?"

I shook my head. Everyone else was slowly waking up.

"Huh?"

"Is that the door?"

"Where am I?"

I shot my father a grave look. "Are the police still outside?"

He nodded. "They should be," he replied. "Whoever this is . . . they let him through."

I tumbled off my spot on the couch and got to my feet. Together, Dad and I walked to the front door. Whoever was out there was really pounding.

"Nancy?" I heard a familiar voice calling. "Nancy? Please? *Estás aqui?*"

My mouth dropped open as I pulled my dad back and threw open the door to find the last face I would have expected.

"Cristobal!"

# THE MISSING LINK

"**N**ancy," Cristobal cried, "I'm so sorry to bother you at this hour. But I had to see you. I had to speak to you."

I backed up. "Cristobal, come in, come in," I said, leading him into the foyer and closing the door behind him. "Dad, this is Cristobal Arrojo, our host at Casa Verde. Cristobal, this is my dad."

Cristobal nodded politely. "Mr. Drew, nice to meet you."

"Likewise." My dad looked a little confused by Cristobal's arrival, but not in a bad way. "Please, come in. We have some guests in the living room who will be happy to see you."

We walked into the living room, and I could hear Bess and George gasp.

"*Cristobal?*" George asked after a moment. "Am I seeing things? Am I still dreaming?"

He laughed. "No, *mi amiga,* it is really me. I took the first flight from San Juan."

I stepped behind Cristobal, gesturing for him to sit down. "Let's all have a seat," I suggested. "And Cristobal, you can tell us what brings you here."

After a couple minutes, we were all settled—sleepy, but awake—on the couches, sipping tea that Ned had made for us all. Expectantly, we all turned to Cristobal, eager to hear his story.

"*Bueno,*" said Cristobal, "the truth is, I am here because of my brother. After talking to you, Nancy, he broke down. He called for me to come to the hospital immediately; he had much to tell me."

I felt prickles down my spine. "Enrique told you everything?" I asked.

Cristobal nodded. "*Everything.* He told me what you had told him, how someone had threatened you, taken your friend. He told me how frightened he was that Cassandra would turn on our family, that even more people would get hurt."

My dad nodded. "Why don't you start at the beginning?" he asked. "What did Enrique tell you about this Cassandra Samuels?"

Cristobal's face darkened. "*Sí*. Cassandra was no stranger to me, you understand—Enrique and I met with her two years ago when we had the idea to create Casa Verde. It was going to be so beautiful—a beautiful resort, but a resort for the earth, as well. We wanted the buildings to be completely green, to live in harmony with nature. Cassandra told us she could help us achieve that, through Green Solutions."

I nodded. "And then what happened?"

Cristobal sighed. "Well, I was very busy with the business end of things, you understand. So my brother agreed to work directly with Cassandra and to oversee Green Solutions as construction began." Cristobal took a sip of tea and grimaced. "At the time, I believed it was all going according to plan. But last night—tonight?—no, last night, Enrique told me the truth." He paused again and then said quietly, "He says he fell in love with Cassandra."

*"What?"* I cried, then immediately felt embarrassed for blurting it out. But then I realized that George had asked the same question, and Bess looked just as amazed as I felt.

"It's true," Cristobal said, looking right at Bess, George, and me. "At first I was amazed as well. He hid it from everyone. We all believed he was still hung up on . . ." He paused, awkwardly rubbing his hand over his face. "You understand, we thought he still had feelings for my wife."

My father looked at me in surprise, but it was true. When we had only been at Casa Verde a few days, we learned that Enrique had once been in love with Cristobal's current wife. In fact, Juliana believed he still loved her. At one point, I had been convinced that Juliana was responsible for the strange happenings at Casa Verde, because she was trying to sabotage her uncle to get back at him for stealing her father's true love. At the time, it had seemed like a sordid discovery, but now, with everything that had happened, it seemed such an innocent thought—almost naive.

Bess frowned. "What about the letters on Enrique's computer?" she asked. Juliana had shown us love letters that her father had saved on his computer; we had believed them to be meant for Cristobal's wife. "Were they for Cassandra, then?"

Cristobal nodded. "That's exactly right." He sighed. "He wrote her hundreds of letters and e-mails over their two-year relationship. He believed they really cared about each other. He was actually considering moving to America with Juliana to be closer to her."

*Hmm.* "So—what happened with the construction of Casa Verde?" I asked.

Cristobal looked uncomfortable now. "This is

what my brother finally confessed to me last night," he admitted. "When it came down to actually planning the resort—after they had been romantically involved for a few months—Cassandra proposed to him the idea of taking some, well, she called them *shortcuts*." He smiled warily. "Substituting lesser quality, less 'green' fixtures for the high-quality ones we'd approved. He says he didn't want to do it at first, but she assured him it would be totally safe—no one would ever notice. And what's more, she promised to split the money she would save with him. She even suggested they could use it to buy a home together in America—and to fund Juliana's college education."

I shook my head. "So he went along with it?"

Cristobal met my eyes for a moment, then nodded. "He did," he agreed. "He says he didn't fully understand the extent of what they were doing. In many cases, he thought it was a matter of choosing a less-green fixture to replace a top-of-the line one; he didn't realize that they were actually using shoddy, substandard equipment. And he never realized that Cassandra was changing the whole design for the resort—channeling the waste into the river, for example."

Everyone was quiet for a moment. I think we were all—those of us who knew him, at least—stunned by what Enrique had done. He seemed like such a sweet, quiet, well-meaning man. And he had helped destroy his brother's dream.

"Anyway," Cristobal said finally, "about three months ago, Cassandra stopped returning Enrique's e-mails. He began to panic. He kept calling her, but she would never pick up the phone and never return his calls. Finally he got her on the phone after weeks of trying. He asked her what was going on—why she was ignoring him—and she said she'd found someone else. He was heartbroken, but he was also racked by guilt over what they had done. He told her that he couldn't live with it anymore—we still had a couple months before the resort opened, and he believed there was time to come clean to me and fix everything. But Cassandra told him if he did that, she would have him sent to prison for the rest of his life. She had recordings of their conversations, e-mails, and letters that all made clear that Enrique was just as responsible for the shoddy construction as she was. She told him she had connections, and that if he came forward, she would see to it that he took all the blame. Worse, she threatened to hurt Juliana."

I gasped.

Cristobal nodded. "That's right. That's when Enrique backed off. He agreed not to say anything, and to let the resort opening go on as planned." He paused. "You know the rest."

Again, everyone in the room was quiet, letting this information soak in. After a few seconds, Cristobal spoke again.

"Enrique said," he began, "that this last week has been the worst of his life. He could see what was happening—that someone had caught on to the ecological abuses and was trying to bring that to the surface while the reporters were there. He said he hoped that whoever it was would eventually give up, but obviously that didn't happen. And then when you got involved, Nancy, and started investigating, everything got ramped up. Suddenly people were getting hurt—or someone was trying to hurt them. He was terrified, because he knew Cassandra was behind it, and he knew that she wouldn't stop until the threat to her business was gone. He kept calling and e-mailing her, begging her to stop the assault, but she wouldn't even answer him. He was so shaken up, he began tape-recording his conversations with her, thinking that they would become useful to the police if anything happened to him."

I looked at my friends. "So this is the missing link: Enrique was working with Cassandra; that's how she got involved with Casa Verde. Right before we came to Costa Rica, Sara figured out the truth, and spent the first few days of our tour trying to prompt us to find out the truth too. But when I started investigating, Enrique inadvertently tipped Cassandra off to what was going on, thinking she was responsible for Sara's early assaults—then Green Solutions swept in."

Hildy nodded slowly. "And all of the later attacks were people working for Cassandra!"

"Right," I agreed.

George piped up, "Then of course, when we got home, and Cassandra realized you were home—she wanted to get rid of you immediately."

Cristobal sighed, rubbing his temples. "Exactly," he said. "Nancy, I am so sorry. I can't apologize enough. Enrique is racked with guilt over what's happened to you—what's happened to everyone. But he doesn't know how to stop it. Cassandra is simply too powerful. I was nervous even leaving him back in Costa Rica, afraid that she would learn that he had told us the truth, and want revenge."

I stood up. "That's why we have to stop her," I insisted. "None of this will stop until we can find her, get Hannah back, and get her put away for all of this!"

"But how?" asked Bess. "We don't know where she is. We don't even know where she *could* be."

Cristobal cleared his throat. "Enrique did give me one bit of information that might come in handy." He looked at me. "She has a summer cottage I guess they spent time at once—on a lake. I believe he said it was called Goose Lake."

I looked at my father. Goose Lake was about eighty miles to the east. We could be there in less than two hours!

But my dad was already on his feet, his tea forgotten on the coffee table. "Let's go," he said simply.

# 13

## SHOWDOWN

**N**inety minutes later on the dot, my dad was pulling his car into an isolated driveway near Goose Lake. "This is it," he observed.

I was riding in the front seat; Bess, George, and Ned had all crammed into the back. Cristobal was right behind us, riding with Hildy. We all had our eyes peeled to get a good look at this summer cabin—and, we hoped, some sign that Cassandra had been there.

"That has to be her car," my father observed, taking in a hybrid SUV with the license plate GRNSOLU. "She must be here."

I felt my pulse speed up. We were here early in the morning, so I hoped we might be able to ambush

Cassandra without her hearing us. But still, the thought of what she might have done to Hannah, and just knowing how dangerous she was, made me shiver in the early morning cool air.

We parked, and slowly, quietly got out of Dad's car. A few yards away, Hildy and Cristobal did the same. We all looked at one another. Finally Dad nodded. "Let's go," he whispered.

The cabin was modest, a one-story box with cedar shingles. We slowly approached the door, which was flanked by two large windows with filmy white curtains. Inside, from what I could see at least, it was quiet and still dark; there were no signs of activity. I peered into what looked like a small living area. I hoped Cassandra was still asleep in her bedroom.

We all stood on the stoop. Dad glanced at all of us, nodded again, and then pounded hard on the door.

For a moment there was no response, but Dad kept pounding. Finally there were sounds of movement from within. After a few seconds, someone emerged into the living area, wearing a bathrobe. I spotted her long red hair and realized it was Cassandra! I took a deep breath. Did she have Hannah in there? Was Hannah okay?

Cassandra ran to the front door, pausing to look out the windows. When she saw who was standing outside—that *all of us* were standing outside—her face paled visibly and she stopped. My father pounded on the door again.

"Go away!" she shouted. "This is private property! I'll call the police!"

I shook my head, meeting her eyes through the window. "You know who I am and you know why we're here," I insisted, shouting. "Let us in or we'll break in!"

While she hesitated, Ned gestured to the window. "See if it's open," he whispered. "It's summer, on the lake. . . ."

He was right. I darted to the window to the right of the door and grabbed the lip, lifting as hard as I could. Sure enough, the window opened—and there was no screen separating me from the inside of Cassandra's cabin! I glanced in, and saw her watching me warily.

"We can all squeeze in this way, I'm pretty sure," I said, keeping my voice low and threatening. "Or you could just let us in the front door."

Cassandra looked like a deer frozen in the headlights. She obviously hadn't been expecting this, and it seemed she had no idea what to do. "This is illegal!" she cried. "You're trespassing!"

"Oh, that's horrible," I replied, faking a look of deep concern. "And you've only lied, kidnapped, committed fraud, broken a bazillion environmental laws, and attempted murder!" I shook my head. "Which one of us do you believe the police will be more worried about?"

Cassandra sighed, shaking her head in frustration. "Fine," she said, walking to the door. "But I don't know what this is about. You can't prove any of the things you just accused me of."

"Can't we?" I asked, backing away from the window and walking back to the door. My father nodded at me, silently approving, though I could tell my boldness was making him a little nervous.

Cassandra unlocked the door, and it swung open. There we were: the seven of us sleep-rumpled, exhausted, and furious; and Cassandra, wrapped in a red velour robe, looking confused and unrepentant. Part of me was amazed that she didn't seem more concerned yet. Did she really think she was that untouchable?

She backed up, letting us step into the cabin, but then just stood there, her arms crossed in front of her chest. We all looked around.

"May we sit?" asked Cristobal finally. He wore a smile, charming as always, though I knew inside he was perhaps the angriest of all of us.

Cassanda just nodded, gesturing to a couch and two small chairs, and we filed into the sitting area. "Let's make this quick, shall we?" she said, seeming to recover from the shock of our arrival. Now she wore a smarmy grin, like she planned to dispose of us posthaste. "I'd like to get some more sleep this morning."

"Very well," my father said, fixing his gaze on her. "Cassandra Samuels, my name is Carson Drew, and I am a lawyer. My friends and I believe you have been part of a huge criminal conspiracy."

Cassandra snorted. "A huge criminal *conspiracy*?" she asked, with an innocent shrug. "Sir, I install low-flow showerheads for a living. What conspiracy might you be referring to?" She glared at us.

I cleared my throat. "Cassandra, we know that Green Solutions is a sham. You convinced Cristobal's brother Enrique to bypass all of the ecologically friendly plans he and Cristobal had requested, and instead you took inexpensive shortcuts—shortcuts that cost the town where Casa Verde is located millions of dollars in environmental damage."

Cassandra laughed. "That was *my* idea, eh? You'd better be careful who you accuse here. It may end up looking very bad for your friend."

Cristobal glared at her. "*Sí*," he said, "we know about your little recordings and letters. But we have some recordings of our own, no?" He reached into his pants pocket and pulled out a tiny tape recorder. As Cassandra's face turned pale, he pressed Play.

Cassandra's voice emerged. *"Enrique, we discussed this. This is what I do for a living, okay? I can't let your little guests get away with murder. If they've caught on to the problems with the resort, I need them to stop snooping around."*

*"Sí,"* said Enrique, *"I understand you want to keep the problems secret, but this is just a young girl, Cassandra. I'm afraid someone is going to get hurt."*

Cassandra snorted. *"That's the idea, Enrique."*

He sighed. *"Cassandra, you can't do this. I agreed to help you build the resort as you wanted—with the substitutions and changes to the original plan—yes. But I never agreed to help you hurt somebody."* He paused. *"I never agreed to help you kill a young girl, mi amor. Please, I think you are not thinking clearly. This is crazy! It has to stop."*

Cassandra laughed. *"Enrique,"* she said, *"you really don't know me at all."*

Then there was the click of Cassandra hanging up.

Cassandra looked stunned. She stared into nothing, her eyes level with the furniture, but unfocused. Then she looked up at Cristobal. "That doesn't prove anything," she said, but her voice was weak.

Cristobal sighed and shook his head. "Doesn't it?" he asked. "I think it proves that you tried to kill Nancy. And that you did so to hide what you and Enrique really built at Casa Verde."

Cassandra's face changed then. Suddenly she looked furious. She glared back at Cristobal. "That may be right," she said, "but if I'm guilty of breaking environmental laws at Casa Verde—and I'm not saying I am—then so is your brother! He knew everything I was installing and not installing. You were too naive to notice."

George broke in, sounding disgusted: "We get that," she said, shaking her head impatiently. "That's your MO—how you operate. You partner with someone who hired you and make *them* agree to the shoddy construction and environmental shortcuts, taking it little by little, starting with seemingly innocent things and moving up to the bigger, more dangerous things." Her eyes narrowed. "Then you keep evidence of the person agreeing to those changes, and you hold it over their head when things get really bad and out of control. When they try to change their minds, you say, 'Oh, but I have this recording of you.' Then you threaten them, just like you threatened Enrique by saying you would hurt Juliana!"

Cassandra shrugged, her cool demeanor coming back. "I may have said something like that. I really can't recall."

"Oh, you did," Cristobal said darkly, pulling a bunch of papers out of his jacket. "Look here—

an e-mail from you to Enrique. Shall I read it?"

Cassandra nodded, but again, her cool demeanor seemed to be crumbling. I could see fear in her eyes.

Cristobal picked up the first piece of paper, a computer printout. "'Enrique, I must demand that you stop calling me, and stop harassing me. What is happening now must continue. I cannot allow anyone to learn too much about Green Solutions and what we do here. It's simply too dangerous. You asked if I was willing to kill, Enrique. I think what I have done so far proves that I'm willing to do whatever it takes to get the job done. Sending down that TV crew—that was the ultimate distraction. Now the real show begins. And I think your young guests may not live to see the ending.'"

Cassandra looked truly scared now. She held her face firm, but her lip trembled, and the color had gone out of her face again. "I—I," she stammered, suddenly looking around the cabin.

"We have you," said Hildy. "Admit it, Cassandra—we got you. It's over. Now if you'll come quietly with us—"

Hildy's soothing voice was cut off by a huge *crash* as Cassandra suddenly grabbed the coffee table—which was protected by a glass pane—and threw it over onto its side. The glass pane hit the wooden floor hard, shattering into a million pieces. As we all stared at the wreckage, Cassandra suddenly darted around and to the right. Ned bolted after her, trying to get between her and the door, but she grabbed his arm and shoved him—much harder than I would have thought someone of her size could manage—and he lost his balance. But the time he regained it, she was out the door.

*"Ned!"* I screamed. *"Cristobal! Catch her!"*

I was on my feet too, running out the door faster than I could have imagined at this hour, and looking around the woods. There she was—her red robe disappearing into a copse of trees. Without hesitating, I ran after her. I could hear her feet pounding through the dried leaves on the ground, and my own following just behind her.

"Give up, Cassandra!" I shouted, hot on her heels. "I'm going to get you! You're going to pay for what you did to me!"

I was gaining on her as we stumbled through the woods—ten feet away, then five feet, then finally three feet. I could hear Cassandra suck in her breath, knowing what was coming, and I lurched after her, throwing out my arms to grab her bathrobe. Just then, though, I felt my toe catch on something—a root on the ground, covered by leaves! I cried out as I felt myself falling, too fast to right myself, and by the time my elbows hit the leaf-coated ground, she had gotten a huge lead on me. Too much of a lead to close the distance.

I stayed where I was, letting out a deep sigh. She was heading toward the end of the driveway, back to the road. Was she getting away?

That's when I heard a clatter of footfalls in the distance.

*"Freeze!"* I heard. *"Police! Miss Samuels, you're under arrest for fraud, kidnapping, attempted murder . . ."*

I smiled. When Dad and I had called Officer Yang to tell him where we were going, he'd arranged for the local police to wait outside Cassandra's cabin. Say what you will about the River Heights PD—they always come through in the end.

That left just one huge concern. We hadn't seen Hannah inside the cabin, and it was so small, I couldn't imagine that she might have been inside without us hearing any sign of her. I walked slowly back to the cabin, where my father, Ned, and Bess were eyeing something several yards down the driveway.

"Look at that," my father suggested when I caught up to them, "under those trees there."

I followed his gaze. Far enough away to fade into the background, but still definitely on Cassandra's property, was a small pop-up trailer. I glanced at my father.

"You think?" I asked.

He nodded, a twinkle in his eye. "I do," he said.

Walking slowly, nervous to be proven wrong, we approached the trailer. There were no sounds from within, but it was still early—and the trailer was far enough from the cabin that Hannah likely hadn't heard our confrontation.

"Hannah?" I cried when we were just a few yards away. "Hannah! Are you in there?"

There was silence—probably only a few seconds, but it felt excruciating, like the longest silence of my life. Then there was a cry from inside.

"Nancy?" It was Hannah. Then, suddenly, the blinds moved away from the window and I saw her face—worried, but seemingly okay! "Nancy! Carson! Oh my gosh! Help me, please!"

"Are you okay?" asked my father, moving closer with a wrinkle of concern on his brow.

Hannah nodded. "I'm fine. Please, just help me out!"

I felt my body sink with relief. The trailer was locked with a padlock, but within twenty minutes or so, the police had cut it off and Hannah was free. I dove into her arms, giving her a big hug.

"Oh, Hannah, thank goodness! I was so worried."

Hannah hugged me back. "I'm fine, darling. Just

a little shaken up. I'm glad *you're* okay, after what I overheard. . . ."

I sighed, leaning into Hannah and closing my eyes. It was over. . . . Casa Verde . . . Enrique's breakdown . . . and most importantly, Green Solutions' reign of terror.

# CAUGHT GREEN-HANDED

THE NEW YORK GLOBE,
Sunday edition

GREEN-EYED MONSTER:
The making of an eco-criminal

By Hildy Kent and Frankie
Gundersen

CHICAGO—Environmentalists and
businesspeople alike were shocked
yesterday when Cassandra Samuels,
the successful CEO of environmental
consulting firm Green Solutions,

was arrested on a list of charges too extensive to repeat here: It includes fraud, kidnapping, and—most shockingly—attempted murder.

As Samuels's peers watched in shock, a story began to emerge of Samuels's criminal connections (her uncle is Fred Dorano, widely believed to be the head of a Chicago crime family); the extensive damage she has done to the environment at sites worldwide, all under the guise of "green development"; and her bizarre and violent targeting of a young local girl, Nancy Drew, who was the first to smell something eco-unfriendly about Samuels's empire of development.

Drew was vacationing in Costa Rica with her friends Bess Marvin and George Fayne, who won a weeklong vacation at eco-resort Casa Verde at a local environmental fair, when she became aware that, as Marvin puts it, "Casa Verde wasn't so verde after all." Her investigations led to some startling revelations about Green

Solutions' business plan. It also led to
a series of attacks, both in Costa Rica
and at home in River Heights, that
Drew was lucky to survive. . . .

"Now *this* . . . ," Bess said with a sigh, sipping an organic ginger-apple juice as she lounged by the freshwater pool on a wooden lounge chair made from sustainable materials, "is relaxing."

I sighed in agreement, putting down my book and snuggling deeper into my own comfy, upholstered lounge chair. It was a couple months after Cassandra Samuels's arrest, and we were back at Casa Verde, at Cristobal's insistence. Ever since Cassandra had been caught, he had been apologizing profusely to Bess, George, and me for all the danger I'd been put in. Finally he offered to host us back at the resort— which was undergoing extensive renovations to become *truly* green. Remembering how much we'd loved Casa Verde, and how much *more* we would have loved it if we hadn't been trying to get to the bottom of the series of attacks while we were there, we happily agreed.

George sat up in her chair. "Oh, look," she said lazily, "here comes Sara."

I sat up too. Sara, the veterinary assistant who

had originally blown the whistle on Casa Verde's environmental shortcuts, had fully recovered from the ant attack we'd witnessed on the last day of our original trip. She seemed utterly happy with the way things had turned out here. Cristobal had been endlessly supportive of her, and although he didn't condone the pranks she'd pulled to focus our attention on the resort's environmental abuses, he understood and was grateful for her dedication to the environment and all the plants and animals that called Casa Verde home. It was, after all, why he had hired her in the first place.

"Hey Sara," I called, and her face lit up as she jogged over.

"Cristobal told me you would be here," she enthused. "I'm so sorry, Nancy, to hear about what you went through in Chicago. But I'm so grateful for what you did. We're going to be a real eco-resort now!"

I nodded, gesturing at the gorgeous pool with its waterfalls, natural plants, and organic juice bar. "It looks like it's really coming along!"

Sara nodded. "We're about three months out from being fully complete. But of course, Cristobal wanted you all to come as soon as possible."

Cristobal was running the resort in its recovery phase. Many familiar faces were still here: Sara and

Alicia, the head veterinarian, among them. We'd also spoken to Violeta, the resort nurse, and Pedro, the driver of the biodiesel van Cristobal used to transport guests all over the country.

"Well," Sara said with a smile, "I have a bird with a broken wing to check on. But I'm sure I'll see you later."

Bess grinned. "We're here all week!" she said happily.

After a few more minutes of lounging, I heard footfalls nearby and another familiar voice. *"Nancy!"*

I sat up. "Juliana!" I would know that voice anywhere.

Juliana was beaming as she ran over to the pool, still wearing her school uniform, her bag still on her shoulder. "I'm so glad to see you," she gushed, looking from me to Bess to George. "I can't thank you enough for what you did, Nancy. By catching Cassandra and getting her hauled off to jail, you really improved my father's health, and now my family is facing the future together."

I smiled. "Oh, Juliana. You're so welcome. I'm sorry you had to go through what you did to get here."

George asked, "How's your dad?"

Juliana smiled. "Better," she said. We all knew that Enrique was recovering well from his breakdown at the hospital; he was talking again, and while he still

142

clearly felt a lot of guilt, he was getting on well with his family and had been released to go home.

"We're seeing a counselor," Juliana went on. "My father and I go twice a week, and Cristobal comes on weekends."

"How's that going?" asked Bess.

Juliana shrugged. "Pretty good," she said. "I mean, it's hard, getting over what my dad did. But I think I'm realizing that he did it out of love—he really wanted a better life for me. And he and Cristobal are working through their issues too. I don't know if they'll ever go into business together again, but they're acting like brothers now, and that's all that matters to me."

I smiled. "And the charges against him have been dropped, right?" I asked.

"Well, not exactly," Juliana explained. "He made a deal with local law enforcement for a reduced sentence, in exchange for giving them inside information about what Cassandra did at Casa Verde." She paused. "He doesn't have to go to jail, but he will do community service. He said he's actually looking forward to it—having some time to think before figuring out what to do next."

I nodded. "Great."

Just then, Bess stood up and grabbed the aluminum can she'd been drinking from. She walked over to a nearly hidden collection of recycling bins and trash cans, all camouflaged by reclaimed wood walls. As we watched, she dangled the can over the *trash* receptacle.

"*Bess!*" I cried, at the same time Juliana and George cried out too. "You have got to be kidding me!"

Bess just giggled, an impish smile on her face. "I just wanted to make sure we'd learned our lesson here," she said, before tossing the can into the *recycle* bin.

George groaned. "Did we ever!"

I laughed. "That's right, Bess—I think your idea to bring us to the environmental fair did more to change the way we think about the earth than you ever could have guessed!"